D1617508

CHAPTER ONE

Robert Morrison Neal stood across the driveway to get a better view of the large house he had spent three solid months of intense physical work helping to renovate.

Damn, it looked good.

The massive house had been built years before, but hadn't been lived in for a couple of years before he bought it. It was too isolated from neighbors for many people, even though it was just a few miles from the little town of Spring Creek, Arkansas. For other people, it was too much effort, or too costly to restore. The property came with a hundred acres of forest; mostly hickory, ash, and the massive white oak trees.

He had asked a cousin, Kamon Youngblood, to redesign the structure to modernize and upgrade everything to make it into a comfortable home. Kamon, a gifted architect, suggested a wider wooden porch to wrap around the front and the side of the two story structure, new windows and doors, and refinishing the wooden exterior. The exterior of the house was built from white oak tree, a hardwood native to the area. Kamon had also designed a dream kitchen with pecan cabinets, a huge island with seats, and shiny new appliances throughout. All other rooms in the large house had been modernized, even the apartment a former employee used extending off the kitchen.

When it was time for the interior decorating, Bob was in his own element as color was at the heart of his profession. He had chosen soft earth tones mingled with blues and greens throughout the house to give the huge, high ceiling rooms a warmer feeling. He had taken his collection of furniture out of storage, then bought complimentary pieces over the internet to furnish the home he meant to live in for a long time. He smiled as he reviewed his property. This home was for him. What he wanted and was comfortable with in this new life he had chosen.

Jennifer would have hated it. She liked the sleek modern style with lots of grays and blacks with sharp edges of light. And he had spoiled her unreservedly, giving her what she wanted. Anything. Everything. Whatever it took to make her happy. And it had almost robbed him of his soul when she died.

Shaking his head to clear the memories, he glanced toward the little house of his only employee, Hank Bond. One of the conditions to buy the property had been to keep the middle-aged man employed for a year. Since he was unsure of what this new venture in moving would require, he had readily agreed. A smart, unplanned move for which he was grateful.

Hank was a gem, knowing what had to be done, and doing it. He took care of the horses and did other general work around the place, even cooking some of the meals they shared as they became very good friends.

The barn was in good condition to stable the two horses that had come with the property. His plans were to buy a few more horses, ranch a little, and try to have a semi-normal life. Along with the horses, the property came with a mama barn cat, her newborn kittens, and a huge mongrel dog name Hugo.

Thinking of Hugo brought the realization that he heard a deep barking from around the bend of the road in front of the house. A panicked bark. If that clueless dog found another porcupine, he was going to ... take him back to the vet, he admitted to himself. Maybe Hugo had found something harmless, he hoped, beginning to jog toward the alarmed barking sound.

Hugo sat on the side of the road in front of two small children who were standing protectively between Hugo and a huddled body on the ground. As Bob jogged up, the tiny girl stepped forward with her right hand holding a large stick.

"Don'cha come any closer," she demanded. "I'll hit you with this stick."

Bob glanced at the little boy with the distinctive features of a Down Syndrome child, staring wide-eyed at him. Bob sat back on his heels beside Hugo to make himself the same height as the little girl.

"Hi, my name's Bob and that's Hugo," he said softly pointing to the dog. "What's yours?"

"My name's Elizabeth, but people call me Lizzie. That's Sammy," she pointed at the little boy. "And that's Mommy," she said, pointing to the unmoving woman laying on the ground. "Are you a bad man?" Lizzie asked narrowing her eyes. "Cause this stick can hurt you."

"No, I'm not. I'm a very good man," he said slowly. "It looks like your mommy may need some help though. I'm going check her so that I can see what she needs."

Kneeling, Bob gently lifted the edge of the ragged coat from the mother's shoulders, noting the bloodstained clothing. His breath caught in his throat as he saw the bloody, swollen face. "Easy, it's okay," he reassured the woman softly. "I'll call an ambulance ..." he started to say.

"Please, please no ambulance. He'll kill all of us." A small hand reached through the sleeve of the ragged coat to clasp his arm. "Promise no ambulance. Please, please," she begged, her voice breaking.

"Shh, shh. Its all right. Okay, no ambulance for right now. I'll call a friend to help you get to my house. My house is just around that bend in the road," he explained softly. He didn't know if she heard him or not as she slid into unconsciousness.

Quickly hitting speed dial, he said, "Deke, I need your help. It's an emergency. Bring Brenna. I found an injured woman and two small children at the bend of the road just before the house."

"We're on our way. We'll leave the kids here with Patty." The line went dead. Never one to ask questions in an emergency, Deke Paxton could be counted on during any crisis. And Brenna, a distant cousin of his, was a healer extraordinaire, the best physician anyone could know. Someone with very special skills.

"Some friends are coming to help carry your mom up to my house," he carefully explained to Lizzy. "Deke's a good guy too. And his wife is coming, she's a doctor," he explained carefully. "They'll help your mommy."

"Ok," the little girl agreed slowly, laying the big stick on the ground. "Mommy does need help, she's hurt. And Sammy doesn't talk, and if you make fun of him, I'll beat you up," promised the little gingered-haired girl, her face fierce with determination.

"No one should make fun of other people," pronounced Bob firmly. "That's wrong and rude."

"Is 'rude' one of them words only adults can say? Cause it's mean too. Some people make fun of Sammy, and I want to hit them. And I'm not sorry."

Bob was unsure what to say next when Deke's large black truck slide to a stop near them.   Brenna immediately hurried from the truck carrying a small black bag. Kneeling beside the unconscious woman, she checked the woman's breathing then run her hands slowly over her ribcage. Closing her eyes, she carefully ran her hands over the rest of the body.

Looking up first at Deke, then at Bob, she murmured, "Her breathing is shallow, but that's because she may have bruised ribs, but no punctures. Her legs seem okay, but we'll have to use butterflies or stiches on some of the cuts. Her left arm is badly bruised, but I don't feel that it is broken. There's a lot of seeping wounds and dried blood. I think it's safe to move her, although it's easier on her before she wakes up. Deke, can you carry her in the truck? Keep her wrapped in the coverings she's in for now."

She turned to the children as Deke carefully lifted the woman and slid into the passenger side of the truck, holding the woman. "We're going to take good care of your mommy," she told the children. "Bob will walk with you to his house just around the bend," she instructed. She quickly got in the driver's seat and drove toward the house.

"Where's they taking mommy?" Lizzie demanded. "I wanta' go with her. She needs us." The little girl started to cry.

4

Sammy looked at her, and tears formed in his eyes.

"Hey guys, it's okay. They're taking your mommy to my house so we can make her better. There's no room in the truck for us all, but my house is right around that bend," Bob pointed in the direction, hoping that would calm down the children for a minute. Taking each child by the hand, Bob walked as rapidly as he could toward the house, Hugo walking beside Sammy.

"What is that?" Lizzie asked, sniffing back tears, tugging him to a stop. "That building up there?"

Bob looked to see what she was asking. His house was the only thing in her sight. From where they were standing, the barn, outbuildings, and Hank's house couldn't be seen.

"Keep walking," Bob encouraged. "Lizzie, that's my house. That's where I live."

"Nope." Lizzie's voice was firm, no nonsense. "Nobody lives in a house that big. Do you live in a school or a store? I never ever saw a building that big."

Deciding that explanations would take time and energy, Bob decided to ignore the questions. "Hurry, let's get to where your mom is. Deke and Brenna may need our help."

Those seemed to be the magic words. The children moved so rapidly that they were almost running, Hugo loping alongside a fast shuffling Sammie.

Hugo bounded up the short stairs onto the porch, with the children right behind him. Bob opened the front door, and they all hurried into the living area.

Lizzie skidded to a stop, her mouth breathing in an "Oh" sound. "This is the biggest room in the world I bet'cha. Is that a fireplace?" Answering her own question, she said, "Yep, it's a fireplace cause its gots wood in there, and its built of rock. Why do you need two couches, and all them chairs and tables?"

Sammie glanced around, but was more interested in playing with Hugo. The dog had rolled over with his feet in the air.

"Hugo wants you to rub his tummy," Bob told the Sammy. When the little boy didn't respond, Bob took one of his tiny star-like hands and moved them over Hugo's tummy. The little boys small slant eyes sparkled as Hugo wiggled.

"Where's mommy?" Lizzie suddenly demanded, looking around for her.

"Brenna? Deke?" Bob called loudly.

"Here," came the muffled reply from one of the nearby downstairs bedrooms. "In here, Bob. And please bring the children. Their mother needs to see them for a moment."

Sammy jumped to his feet to shadow a running Lizzie, as she followed the sound of Deke's voice.

"Momma, oh momma," cried Lizzie, Sammy behind her.

"Easy sweetie, easy," Brenna reached out a hand to stop the children from flinging themselves on their mother's body. "Your mommy's hurt right now, but she wanted to see you, to be sure you're all right," Brenna gave a warm smile to each child.

"You're okay?" asked the woman softly, her one-eyed gaze on the children. "The dog didn't hurt you?"

"Oh no, mama. The dog's name is Hugo, he's big, but he likes to have his tummy rubbed. Sammy does that, huh, Sammy?" At Sammy's nod, she continued, "Momma, this house is bigger than a store. And the fireplace is so big I could stand up in it if I wanted." Then added, "But I don't want to."

Bob had to swallow hard as he stood just outside the room. The woman was an unrecognizable bloody mess. Her hair was matted with blood, stuck together in dirty tangles, one eye swollen completely shut, the other a mere slit of green. Her face was turning a blackish-purple color as was the arm that he could see. Several small cuts appeared to be red and puffy, but were no longer bleeding. The woman seemed to be struggling to stay awake, then with a tiny groan of pain, her eyes slowly closed, and she succumbed to deep sleep or unconsciousness.

Brenna spoke directly to the children. "Lizzie, Sammie, my name is Brenna. I'm a doctor, I take care of people who need care. That's my husband Deke over there," she indicated with a hand wave toward the large man at the back of the bedroom. "And you already know Bob. And I have little children too."

Brenna's eyes held sincerity as she added, "And we're

going to help your momma. I need to check a couple of things still. And Bob, I may want to stay here tonight if that's all right with you, just to be sure that …, that everything's okay".

Deke watched her for a moment as she looked from him, then back to the kids. The large man's eyes warmed with understanding, then replied to Brenna. "Well, while you're being sure, maybe we could raid the refrigerator and get some snacks to eat. Would you like to help me find stuff?" he asked the children.

"Sure. We like to eat snacks, whatever that is," Lizzie stated firmly, taking one of Deke's hands. Sammie took Lizzie's other one. "We'll be back," she told her mother as they walked out.

Moving to the doorway out of Leeann's hearing range, Brenna lowered her voice.

"Bob, her name is Leeann Downey. We've had very little time to talk as she's in a lot of pain, but she says she's fleeing an abusive husband. I've taken pictures just in case she needs them later. She has multiple cuts and bruises. Her arm was dislocated, and her back is still bleeding, that's why she is turned on her side. She didn't want the children to see the bandages covering the lacerations. He beat her with his belt, the buckle, and his fists."

She took a deep breath, "There's also old scars where he must have taken his belt to her back and legs. The indications are that this is not the first time, nor the tenth time he's beat her. You need to know all this as several decisions have to be made. She has sixty-seven dollars and twenty-five cents that she's been able to save over the last two years and no other resources."

Brenna watched Leeann's face as she continued to talk in a low murmur. "She says her husband drinks, and uses opioids mixed with meth. She doesn't know what else. I have given her my promise that I will not take her to a hospital. With the pain and sleeping medications I've given her, she's probably out until the morning, when she can be moved. Then I'll take her and the children home with me for awhile. Deke won't mind."

"Brenna, I know you're working this week for Dr. Farrison.

That means that your helper, Patty, and Deke, would be caring for her, and her children, plus your two. You're not going to be as available as I am. Why would you move her from here?"

Brenna held his gaze for a full minute, saying nothing.

Bob shook his head slightly. "I can handle whatever it is. She and the children can stay here," he said firmly. "Brenna, there's certainly enough room here, and I can change bandages as you know." A fleeting look of sorrow crossed his face, then he stood up straighter.

"Bob, are you sure? It's a big undertaking. I can stay tonight and check in tomorrow night but ...."

"I'm positive," he asserted, falling silent, letting Brenna decide, as she was one of the handful of people who knew his background.

Brenna nibbled on her lower lip in thought as she studied Bob for several moments. "Okay, here's what would work best. There's a retired nurse that I think would be willing to take on short-term nursing duties for a week or so. She's done it several times for me before. She's confidential and motherly. One of the things that this asshole did to Leeann was to also beat her around the pelvic area with his fists and belt. Quit frankly, I think Leeann would be more comfortable with a female nurse doing those duties that some of this is going to require."

"Damn, I liked to get my hands on that Son of ...."

"You'd have to stand in line," Brenna interrupted. "And you would have to hurry before Deke and I got there. But remember, it's only a matter of time until this abusive husband finds out where she is. He'll want her back to take out his anger on. The longer that time is the better, so the less people that know where she is, the more time she has to heal. We can help her deal with some decisions she'll have to make in the future. For now, getting her healed is the goal. Also for now, having full charge of two small, very active children will be more than enough for you to worry about. Lizzie seems to be pretty self-confident," Brenna grinned.

"Ya think?" Bob kidded. "She's threated me with a stick if

I hurt her mother, or was mean to Sammie. I have to admit I like that kid's style."

"Leeann said she was four and a half, and Sammie is seven-years-old. Lizzie's more like four going on forty-four," chuckled Brenna, pushing her long auburn braid to her back. "Catherine's Alexa is about the same age. Let's not arrange a play-date for them – they might take over this part of the state of Arkansas. Our three-year-old son, Brandon, follows Alexa around and just does whatever she tells him to do. She rewards him with cookies. Smart boy," she grinned.

Turning serious, she asked, "Leeann thinks she's leaving here tomorrow, but she won't even be able to get out of bed by then. Besides her pelvic area, her back and left arm are a mass of bruises and cuts when he used the buckle end of his belt on her. And," she added, "she doesn't know how long she was unconscious. Except for her eye, there's no other serious head injuries, although she does have a very mild concussion which is going to require some time to heal."

"How long are you talking about Brenna. For her to heal? Any idea?"

"Three or four days in bed, then rest for several more with frequent naps. Good food, lots of sleep with no activity." She narrowed her grass-green eyes in thought. "And no emotional stress. And don't ask because I don't know how in the hell we're going to manage that. She's sound asleep, lets check the children."

Bob walked into his kitchen behind Brenna. Seated at the breakfast bar was Deke, Lizzie and Sammie with plates of bacon, eggs, and toast in front of each of them. Hank was at the stove with his back to them.

Glancing up, Hank asked. "You all want me to fry up some more eggs or bacon? It won't take but just a minute."

"We're good for now," Deke answered, his eyes focused on Brenna.

Lizzie turned around on her stool when she heard them enter. "Mr. Bob, this is one of those rest-er-runt kitchens I saw in a magazine at the general store once." She pointed to where a grinning Hank stood over the stove with a spatula in his hand. "Mr. Hank says we're having breakfast for dinner, and that we can eat all we want. Can we?" she asked hesitantly.

"Sure," Bob answered. "I love to see people eat. Hey, Hank. Thanks for coming up to help."

"Deke and Lizzie filled me in on some stuff." His smile was grim as he added, "Maybe we can take some gas down the road and get the truck out of the driveway. Lizzie said they run out of gas."

"Lizzie, Sammie," Brenna focused her attention on the children. "Your mommy needs to rest for a few days so she can get better. You're going to stay here with her. Bob and Hank live here, and Deke and I live next door." She didn't tell them that next door was several hundred acres over. "When you finish your snack, I'm going to get you washed up and let you sleep in a room next to your momma."

"I want to sleep with momma," Lizzie whined. Sammie blinked at Lizzie, then screwed up his face to cry too.

Brenna hastily assured them, "Momma hurts right now and needs to sleep by herself. I'm going to rest in a recliner by her bed to be sure she is okay tonight. I'll leave the door open and the light on so you can see us. What did you leave in your truck?" She asked, looking to distract them and to gain information.

"We left momma's quilts that she made. We were wrapped up in them 'cause the truck doesn't have a heater momma said. And it was cold."

"Nothing else?" asked Brenna. "No clothes, or toys?"

"Nope," Lizzie said matter-of-factly. "We had to hurry and leave before he comed back. We had rag dollies mama made, but he burned them last winter."

The adults shared a quick incredulous look.

"There's some t-shirts in the top drawer in the bedroom, if you want to use them," Bob stated. "They might make night shirts. Brenna, you know you can have anything that I have. Oh, except Hugo. We're going to keep him here," he smiled at the children, including them in the decision.

"Yep. We're gonna keep him here," echoed Lizzie. Hugo lay beside the table, probably hoping for dropped tidbits.

"While you put gas in the truck, I'll get Lizzie and Sammie washed up and into bed. Then I need to call Mrs. Hansen," Brenna declared, putting a hand on Lizzie's shoulder to move her toward the bedroom. "Bob, would you share our conversation with Deke and Hank, please?"

CHAPTER TWO

After the kids left the room, Bob filled the other two men on his talk with Brenna, and the choices that had been made. Leeann and the children would remain at Bob's house until she healed, or until some other decisions had to be made. A nurse was going to come to stay to help care for her.

"You're both relatively newcomers here," Hank said slowly. "So neither of you know about the three Downey brothers. Leroy Downey is Leeann's husband, the youngest of the three. They live up on the North Fork, the last out-of-the-way tiny community deep in the mountains.

"The Downey's are all rattlesnake mean, striking out for no apparent reason except that they can. They were young bullies, and now they're hardened lawbreakers. Opioid addicts and who knows what other kind of shit they use. Semi-sober they're malicious, and when they're drunk or high, their cruelty is beyond despicable."

He paused, then continued, "A friend told me they ganged up on a young man in a bar a couple of months ago, and kicked him to death. Then they threatened the entire bar that their families would pay if it wasn't declared self-defense. All the people in the bar knew that the Downey's would absolutely follow through with that threat. They all backed the self-defense story."

"Law enforcement didn't investigate?" asked Deke frowning. "You know I spent years in law enforcement, and ninety-nine percent of officers are honest and want to right wrongs."

"Will Smyth is honest, but he has a large family and a host of other kin. Unless he knows he can get a conviction, he would be stupid to arrest them," Hank explained carefully. "And Smyth's not stupid. He's been the police chief for a long time. Before that he was the sheriff."

"Then informing him of Leeann and the kids hereabouts would be futile, and probably dangerous for her?" asked Bob. "He either can't, or won't, help?"

"Yep it would, and no, he can't. Most people avoid any contact with the Downey's. That's the easiest and safest way. Their father was a moonshiner who competed with his kin for being the nastiest man on that mountain. They followed in his footsteps after he died. They're completely unpredictable and spiteful. I wanted you to know what I've been told. I suspect that they're even worse than I've heard."

"Thanks Hank. Why don't you go back to bed? Deke and I will take some gas down to get the old truck she was driving while Brenna puts the kids to bed."

"Nay. I'm wide awake now. If you can drive the truck up here, I'll make room for it in the back shed by the old tractor. There's a tarp we can cover it with, and a good lock on that shed door. If we have to move it later, that will be easy with the forests behind us."

"Sounds like a plan," grinned Bob. "Thanks again for your help Hank. And you too Deke."

"Hey, I go where Brenna goes. And I'm delighted to do so," he grinned, his eyes shining. "If we need more information about Leeann's situation, I know someone locally that might be able to give us info without getting the law involved. He's rather anti-law," he grinned. "And I have a cousin by marriage that's can be downright scary."

"Yeah, he is. He's a great architect and his designs are awesome, but he can also be intimidating. And intense."

"Actually he shares much of those attributes with you," grinned Deke. "And Kamon has mellowed some with marriage, but he is a force," agreed Deke as he and Hank left the room.

The next morning Mrs. Hansen arrived in an old truck before the sun was fully up. She was a round, middle-aged woman with laugh lines near her eyes, a permed halo of gray hair, and a bright smile on her face. She carried a small suitcase, and a large bag of groceries.

"Morning Hank", she greeted the older man with a pat on the shoulder as he let her in the door. "Still cooking I see."

"Aww Sarah, cooking helps me relax," he drawled, taking the groceries from her. "Besides there's kids here now that need to be fed directly."

"Good morning, Sarah," welcomed Brenna, walking into the room. "Thanks for coming. Dr. Farrison is taking a few days off to spend with his daughter in Canada, so I'm filling in for him. I'm so glad you could help out."

Bob walked in behind Brenna, carrying his coat over his arm. "Good morning. You must be Mrs. Hansen. I'm Bob Neal. We all appreciate you coming to help."

"And you are most welcome, but call me Sarah please," the older woman breathed, her face turning red as she stared at Bob. "Oh Hank, I have several boxes in the back of the truck. Would you bring them in for me?" she asked, tearing her eyes away from Bob Neal for a moment.

At Brenna's questioning look, she explained, "You told me the kids didn't have clothes, toys or anything. I keep some of the grandchildren's clothes at the house along with toys when they visit. Heather is a small size six, and Billy Bob's little boy, Charlie, is size eight. I brought what they had at my house, and then took an early run by Wal-Mart for some things. I'm always doing that so no one will wonder about it."

"Good grief," Bob exclaimed, "You're absolutely amazing. I should have thought of that. Thank you so much," he smiled fully at the blushing woman. "I'll help you carry things in Hank."

Sarah watched Bob walk out, and then waved her hand back and forth across her face as if to cool it. "Whoa, Brenna. That is one beautiful man. Holy Ned, I mean really, really pretty. All that golden skin, black eyes and light blond hair. That big physique with those wide shoulders isn't bad either."

Brenna grinned widely at the flustered nurse.

"Whew," Sarah sighed heavily. "I am not promising that even at sixty-three, well sixty-six if truth be told, that I won't stare or maybe stutter. And once the gals around here see him, there's going to be some hearts that's going to beat faster."

"Bob's an unusual man. I'm used to his looks now, but when he first came here to live, all of us ladies oohed and awed. Privately of course. Now, he's just another sort of distant cousin. And I certainly don't have to remind you about confidentiality in our profession."

"When we decided to enter the medical arena, that was a given. Have to protect patients and everyone else." Sarah's eyes shined as if they shared a secret. Smiling as two young children entered, she said, "Well, well, you must be Lizzie and you must be Sammie."

Lizzie stepped back, just out of reach of Sarah's pats, but Sammie accepted the quick hug with a shy smile.

"I'm Nurse Sarah," she explained warmly to the children. "I'll be staying here to take care of your mama for a few days until she's better."

"Is she nice? To my momma?" asked Lizzie to Brenna, avoiding eye contact with Sarah. "She not gonna get mean to me and Sammie is she? I never knowed a nurse before."

"She's very, very nice," Brenna assured the tiny girl. "Nurses are like doctors, they help
people who are sick." Before she had a chance to continue, Bob and Hank came back into the living area carrying two large cardboard boxes and several large plastic bags.

"Sarah, may I pay ...," Bob asked, his eyes lingering on the clothes in the boxes and seeing new tags on some of the items.

"Nope, I decided a long time ago that my discretionary money would go in my little brown kitchen jar to be used locally and anonymously. It helps a few people and that makes me happy," she smiled.

"Okay, kids, how about some breakfast?" Hank asked, interrupting. "Are you hungry, Sammie?"

"Sammie's always hungry," mumbled Lizzie. "Me too

15

sometimes."

"Do you like pancakes?" he asked. "I make great pancakes that look like Mickey Mouse."

"A mouse? Whose Mickey mouse?" queried Lizzie, frowning as if she should know the answer.

"He's a cartoon character," Bob explained. At Lizzie's still-blank look, he added, "A TV cartoon character."

"I saw a TV once. It was in Mrs. Simmons house. I had to go to the bathroom really, really bad and Mr. Simmons at the store told his wife that I had to go. Mrs. Simmons was watching some people in a big box kissing each other. She told me that it wasn't real, and it was just on TV. Then she took me to the bathroom." She lowered her voice, "It wasn't an outhouse. The bathroom was inside, like here" she whispered. "I went, then she washed my hands and I dried them."

Bob looked at the other adults. They all appeared to be stunned. Sarah Hansen started to say something, but Bob shook his head slightly. It would be best if the Lizzie talked a little at a time. Telling her story her way would get more information. But where in the world had these kids been? No television meant that it was unlikely that there was electrical power, so no television. Or electric lights. Or any modern conveniences. Completely off the grid?

Brenna interrupted his thoughts. "Gotta go start my day," she grinned. "Bob, thanks for going with Deke to get my little car last night. I'll see you all tonight sometime," she added, giving the two children quick hugs.

Nurse Sarah went to introduce herself to her patient and to make sure she didn't need anything. "As soon as you've washed up after breakfast, come and get me. I'll help you find some clothes to dress in," Sarah told the children, nodding toward the large T-shirts they had slept in.

Lizzie and Sammie sat side by side at the long trestle table as Hank gave them each a large pancake with little mickey mouse ears on the side of the round griddlecake. Lizzie told Bob to help Sammie 'smear butter and syrup on his large pancake, cause he don't cut so good'."

Bob and Hank grinned at each other, following Lizzie's exact orders. She managed to cut her pancake in large pieces, although most of them were torn apart with her fork rather than her knife. She stuffed large pieces in her mouth, humming with pleasure at the syrup drenched food.

As soon as Lizzie finished, she hopped down off her chair. Immediately, Sammie put down his half-finished meal and started to follow her.

"Wait up for a minute," Hank requested, picking up Sammie and putting him back on his chair. "Sammie isn't quite finished and he wants to go with you."

"Okay," Lizzie heaved a big sigh. "I forgots to wait. He eats slower than me. Momma says his mouth is littler. And I just gots to see what's in those boxes though."

"While we're waiting let's talk about the foods you like to eat. What do you like?" Bob questioned. When Lizzie stared back at him frowning, he tried another tactic. "Do you like to eat chicken?" Lizzie nodded. "Do you like fried potatoes?" Again Lizzie nodded, "How about fruits, like oranges, apples, and bananas?"

"I like apples but I don't know those other ones."

Bob looked at Hank for help.

With a shrug, Hank asked, "How about I cook what Bob and I like, and you taste everything? If you don't like it, then you don't have to eat it. Okay?"

Lizzie nodded. "Sammie, you about through cause I wants to see what's in those boxes." Sammie wiped his mouth on his baggy t-shirt and hopped off the bench.

"First, we do what Nurse Sarah said and go wash up. You don't want to get syrup all over whatever's in those boxes," Bob reminded them.

Both children run toward the kitchen sink. Bob shook his head toward Hank to stop any objections. Bob pulled a clean dish towel from a drawer and helped each child wash their hands and face, drying them carefully. "There now, let's go very quietly to get Nurse Sarah in case your momma's asleep. First though, we have to thank Mr. Hank for breakfast. Thank you," Bob said to Hank, role modeling the behavior.

"Thank you for breakfast, Mr. Hank. Sammie thanks you too," Lizzie added as she glanced at Bob for approval. She was rewarded with a broad smile which she returned.

They quietly went to the door to peep into the bedroom where their momma and Nurse Sarah were. The nurse put her finger over her lips indicating that they had to be quiet as Leeann was asleep.

"Bob, would you mind staying here? Leeann's restless and I don't want her to wake up with no one here. She's on a lot of medications and might not remember much from last night."

"Sure, I'd be glad to. If you need help with any of those boxes, Hank is out in the kitchen."

Lizzie ran back toward the living room, Sammie following her with Nurse Sarah moving more slowly behind them.

Bob sat down in the straight backed chair furthest from her bed. He could hear Leeann's soft moans in her sleep and see her slight movements as she fought her unseen demons. She lay on her side facing the wall so her back covered in bandages was visible to him. This was the first time he had actually seen her as a person. She was tiny, no more than five feet or a little more. Her head was wrapped in a fluffy towel. He would guess to keep the blood and mess from being uncomfortable until her hair could be washed. Either Brenna or Sarah had washed the blood and dirt from her face and arms.

Leeann gave a low groan as she moved restlessly, as if monsters invaded her sleep. Her thrashing became more agitated.

"Shh, shh, it's okay you're safe," Bob soothed softly. He didn't dare touch her. A strange man's touch might make her react with terror. He tried to keep his voice low and smooth as he assured her, "This is my house. No one is going to hurt you here. Your children are fine. Mrs. Hansen is a nurse and she is taking care of them right now. As soon as you wake again you can see them yourself."

Bob smiled as Leeann's shoulders relaxed. Those were the all-important words. Her children. She had needed to hear that they were not in danger before she could relax enough to sleep or rest.

Watching Leeann, he couldn't stop his thoughts from traveling back to his own past. Jennifer. She had been so young, too young, but she was everything he thought he wanted. Outgoing, fun, and very sexy. Everything he felt he wasn't. She had lived every moment to the fullest, wringing out every pleasure, as if she knew that her time in this world would be short. And he had learned some lessons the hard way.

His thoughts were jerked back to the present with the joyful, but loud, sound from Lizzie. Stepping to the door, he watched Lizzie's excited face as she pulled a sweater over her new jeans, Sarah reminding her to speak more softly.

Hank was helping with the buttons on Sammie's new shirt. Sammie's jeans were a little long for him but the middle fit the soft roundness of his body shape. "There, these fit just right," Hank grinned, cuffing the pant legs and giving the little boy a pat on the shoulder. "You look spiffy," the older man asserted.

Bob kept the door partially open as he joined the delighted group in the living room. Lizzie was practically dancing with hushed excitement as she held up two coloring books with boxes of crayons. On the floor, there were a couple of dump-trucks, small cars, and several soft, well-loved dolls.

Sammie had a thumb firmly in his mouth as he gazed at the stuffed animals beside him. Bob realized that Sammie had no idea he could play with them. Glancing back at Leeann to make sure she was still sleeping, he walked slowly toward Sammie. Crouching beside the little boy, he picked up a soft teddy bear. "These are for you to play with," he explained slowly to Sammie, giving the bear to him.

Sammie held the bear with his left arm, then slowly slid his thumb from his mouth. He clutched the bear to his chest, breathing deeply as he stared at the stuffed toy.

"He's called a Teddy Bear," Bob continued softly, glancing

at Sarah Hansen. "Show Nurse Sarah how soft he is," he encouraged gently guiding Sammie toward her. As soon as he was sure Sammie was okay, he returned to watch over the wounded Leeann.

The vulnerable had to be protected. No matter how you felt, it was your duty and responsibility to obey the ancient laws to protect. To be the Sword and the Shield as the ancient ancestors had vowed.

CHAPTER THREE

Leeann woke up slowly, peering through one swollen eye. Her other eye refused to open. Her entire face stung as if she had been bitten by a horde of insects. She tried to slowly lift her arm but she didn't have the strength.

It took her a moment to orient herself to where she was, or who the woman sitting knitting in the chair was. Mrs. Hansen, a nurse. That doctor, Brenna Something, had explained that she was going to call her. She gave a slight gasp as with memory came the overwhelming fear of Leroy and his brothers finding her. Panicked, she tried to sit up but the pain and stiffness made her fall back into place with a wincing groan.

"Whoa, whoa honey. Lay still. You slept all day yesterday. You're sore and badly bruised everywhere, but you're going to be all right. Lizzie and Sammie are outside feeding the chickens with Hank and Bob."

"No, no, you don't understand. I have to leave. I couldn't have slept that long," Leeann insisted, disbelief in her voice. "The kids are outside? No! Please. No one can see them. He'll hurt them. Please," she begged.

"Shh now. No one's going to hurt anybody," Nurse Sarah soothed. "No one is going to come down that road either. There's an iron gate out there that's locked. I guess it was open when you came through, but Bob says normally he keeps it locked. He likes his privacy. And your old truck is out of sight."

"The kids.... They're okay? Is Lizzie being good?" She gave a deep sigh. "She can sometimes be a handful. Sammie's good I know."

21

"They're both fine. Let's get you into the bathroom. Then we can see if you can stand to take a shower or bath. Or if we need to wait until tomorrow."

"A bath would be wonderful," Leeann struggled to pull herself upright, fighting through the pain and nausea.

"Then a bath it is," Mrs. Hansen smiled, gently helping her sit upright. "Let me fill the tub and put some special aloe soap and some meds in it. You'll feel better after a long soak."

Leeann sat on the edge of the bed holding onto the sides as her head swam. She could do this. She had to do this. The kids needed her healthy so they could leave and hide, somewhere Leroy and his brothers couldn't find them.

"That bathroom is something" exclaimed Mrs. Hansen coming back to help her into the bathroom.

Leeann held back a gasp of pleasure as she entered the large bathroom. The bathroom was tiled in blues, greens and turquoise, each flowing gently into the next set of tiles. Turquoise towels and silver accessories made the bath a beautiful sensual painting. Leeann tried to memorize how the colors all flowed one into the other. If she ever had the opportunity, she promised herself a quilt in colors just like the bathroom tiles.

A large galvanized tub was all that had been available for the last couple of years, and it had to be filled and emptied by hand. After bathing the two children in the old tub, she often gave herself a washing all over in the water. The kids needed bathing almost every day as they played in the dirt around the old house in the woods.

Nurse Sarah helped her into the large bathtub's frothy water, putting a padded board behind her back. The nurse carefully washed her hair and rinsed it twice with a hand held shower spray. She let Leeann relax in the hot soapy water for several minutes. The water had stung a little at first, then it seemed that the warmth seeped into her very skin, absorbing some of the pain. Afterward, Sarah helped Leeann step out of the tub and dry off.

"I'm going to put you in one of Bob's soft shirts after I

blow dry your pretty hair," Sarah smiled. "Then you can eat a little of my homemade chicken soup. Its delicious, even if I do say so myself. The kids should be inside in a few minutes, so let's get you dressed and in bed."

Docilely, Leeann followed the nurse's instructions. She was so tired and sleepy that she felt numb all the way to her toes. The nurse used a hand-held machine to blow a warm wind through her hair to dry it, which was heavenly.

Afterward Sarah brought her a large cup of thick chicken and noodle soup. Leeann ate every bite before almost tumbling backward in sleepy exhaustion. Her eyes had just closed when Lizzie and Sammie rushed in.

"Momma, oh momma. We fed the chickens and the rooster tried to chase us but Mr. Hank stopped him. And the big horse's name is Big Ben and the littler one is Patsy, and there's a big bunch of cows, and Mr. Bob let us pet the baby kittens, and the mamma cat's name is Mitzi, and the kittens are too little to have a name and...," She ran out of breath.

Hank chuckled from the doorway. "Leeann, I'm Hank. I work for Bob, and right now I'm helping him out with your children. They've been having fun. I'm glad you're looking better. Still peaked though," he added honestly.

"Thank you for helping," said Leeann yawning. "I seemed to be so sleepy, I can't keep my eyes open."

"We'll take right good care of your children," Hank assured her. "And I'd better start dinner. Would you two like to help me?" he asked the children.

"Yep. I want to help," Lizzie told him, following him out of the room with Sammie two steps behind her.

"Sorry," Leeann apologized to Sarah, her voice slurring. "I can't seem to stay awake." She let her eyes drift shut.

Several hours later, Bob came in to relieve Sarah so she could have dinner. He sat down beside Leeann's bed and glanced at the sleeping woman to assure himself she was okay before he started to read his book.

"Holy hell," he whispered as his breath caught. Leeann's

long hair was draped over the pillow and spilled down her back. The hair spread out on the pillow was a riot of mingled colors. The colors were an unreal mix of strands of blonde, dark auburn, and platinum. It was as if the Creator's mind couldn't decide between the colors, so had blended them together.

It was the most beautiful mingling of colors he had ever seen or imagined. A blend of colors merging into each other, yet separate and each distinct. The auburn and blonde was a swirl of colors, but the platinum was like highlighting a night sky playing tag with lighting bolts. Or the sunset over the pier of Key West, Florida just after dusk.

His hands moved involuntarily as he reached to touch the radiant mix of color spreading across the white pillow. Realizing his reaction, he quickly withdrew his wayward hands back into his lap. He itched to touch the unusual mix of colors, to spread each strand to it's fullest length. It would be difficult to capture the shades on canvas, but it was glorious to view.

Sarah came back in, followed by Brenna. Brenna and Deke had visited every evening after work, Brenna to assure herself that her patient was in full recovery mode.

"While you're busy Brenna, I think I'll put the kids to bed after I read them a story," Bob explained, hiding his awed reaction to Leanna's hair color. "Then Hank said he needed to talk to us. He just got back from an afternoon in town."

Two stories and a glass of water later, Bob finally had Lizzie to asleep. Sammie had zonked out in the matching twin bed as soon as his head had touched his pillow. Bob returned to the dining area to meet the group. Leeann was also sleeping, so Sarah joined them too.

"I wandered around town some this afternoon, trying to talk to as many friends as I could. Gossiping actually," Hank grinned. "Long story short, the Downey brothers know that Leeann is in the area. Old man Hawkins told me that one of their friends had seen Leroy's old truck pull off into some trees. The friend been drinking so all he could remember was that he thought he saw it on some road south of town."

24

He stopped for a moment then continued. "Leroy Downey is telling everyone that he's worried about his wife. He says that she took his daughter and stole his truck so she must have gone completely off the rails. He's gone to Judge Caukins, and I guess Chief Smyth is going to be forced to investigate." Hank paused for a moment. "Leroy and his brothers are raisin' so much hell that they're going to eventually find out where she is. They say they're going to search every house south of Spring Creek until they find her, or find out where she's gone."

"That can't possibly be legal," observed Deke.

"It isn't," agreed Hank. "But the rules are being bent because Leroy says that his wife fell, hit her head and is now crazy. They have to find her for her own good."

"Then we'll plan to be searched," Bob said in a hard firm voice. "I was hoping that we would have more time for Leeann to heal which would give us other options." Narrowing his eyes in thought he asked, "How long do you think it will take them to get to our place?"

"The Chief says that he's going to do it systematically, starting in the areas closest to town and working further out. So I would guess about two or three days, maybe a day or so longer."

"Then the first thing to do is to move Leeann and the kids to a safer place, at least temporarily. And to somehow get rid of Leroy's old truck," Deke said.

"I can take care of the truck problem," volunteered Hank. "There's a grove of trees about a mile back of here that's completely hidden from any road but there's a trail lower down to get there. I'll take it up there and leave it. No one would be able to find it. I may have trouble finding it again myself," he grimaced.

"Leeann could come to our house, but they'll come there too I suspect," Brenna said. Catching Deke eye, she murmured. "Lets think about it, but table it for tonight."

Deke shook his head slightly at Bob not to say anything more. Hank bid them all good night and walked quickly toward his cabin. Sarah returned to her charge and to the small bed where she slept near her patient.

Lifting an eyebrow, Deke asked, "Better idea, Brenna?"

"Actually no, not a better idea about moving Leeann. But there is something wrong. I pick up a weird feeling from Leeann when I touch her. It happened even the first time when she was so injured laying in the driveway."

"What kind of weird feeling? Is something else wrong with her? Internal damage?" Deke asked slowly.

"No, nothing like that. Physically she's in good shape under the circumstances. She's underweight of course, but that's probably from a lack of adequate food. She's healing, both from the beating she took, and the older, deeper bruises. Truthfully, I just don't know why. The vibes I'm getting are strange. This probably makes no sense to you, but she doesn't feel normal to me. When I touch her, something is off, not right somehow, yet not physically wrong," Brenna frowned in frustration.

"I know that her background and beatings happened as she has said. It's backed up by a four-year-old who is incapable of keeping a secret, especially Lizzie. No, it's something else. I've never had this happen before and it's leaving me exasperated." Brenna frowned, "I hate feeling out of control. Give me a chance to talk it over with my sisters before I jump to conclusions."

Both men were silent. Bringing in Catherine and Raina Ramsey put another layer into the picture. An unknown, strange factor. Brenna must think the situation serious to bring out the big guns of Catherine and Raina.

Catherine Ramsey was the chosen clan leader of the ancient tribal clan of Scots/Native Americans. Their small community had lived for years in an isolated wildlife sanctuary high in the Ozark Mountains of Arkansas. She needed the privacy and isolation of Shadow Valley for the protection it gave her, and her hereditary gift of Second Sight.

Raina Ramsey, the youngest sister, also lived in Shadow Valley. She was recognized as being able to organize a small country with little effort before sunset on any given day, along with some uncanny hereditary abilities.

Brenna, the middle sister, had chosen to live on a horse

ranch with her husband Deke near the little town of Spring Creek. A physician, she practiced medicine part–time with the local physician, Dr. Farrison, and was available to the Spring Creek Hospital when needed.

Bob nodded his head along with Deke. Brenna knew exactly what she felt she needed, and if she needed to consult with her sisters, then that's exactly what she should do.

"And the immediately problem? Any ideas on where we can move Leeann and the children?" Bob asked.

"Of course I could fly them anywhere. To the ranch in Texas, or to anyplace really," Deke stated. "What are you thinking Brenna?" he asked frowning at his fiery-haired other half, her hip cocked and her facial expression fierce.

"I don't think she can be moved right now without causing some internal damage. Between her mild concussion and deeply bruised ribs, she's developed an infection from the injuries to her pelvic area. I need to keep monitoring the infection as does Sarah. We need to buy some time so Leeann can heal."

"Hmm," she murmured, her green eyes dancing, "I think the best thing to do is quarantine Bob with measles."

Both men looked stunned and started to laugh.

"Measles is perfect," she insisted, her voice taking on a serious tone. "The United States eradicated the disease twenty years ago, but there's been a recent outbreak in several states. A lot of the people in some of the more isolated places have not been vaccinated. I doubt that the people where Leeann is from have been either," Brenna smiled. "Hank will get rid of the truck. I will quarantine Bob, which is legally done by a physician. Done deal," she grinned, rubbing her hands together.

"Brenna, I had the measles vaccine when I was a child," Bob protested. "I can't get the measles."

"I know that and you know that, but the town people do not know that. This will work," she insisted. "The only other thing we will have to do is to keep the kids from playing outside, and from spreading their toys everywhere. That'll be the hardest of all."

Bob thought it over for a couple of minutes. "Actually Brenna, that might work well. I'm going to hate it but ...."

Deke agreed, "For now it's a good plan and so off-the-wall that it might be believable."

"Hugo can be a big help with keeping the kids occupied. And the TV. I think that with some videos that it could be managed pretty well. There's also a TV in the bedroom where the kids have been sleeping in case its needed. And we need to let Sarah and Hank in on the plan," grinned Bob.

When asked, Sarah thought it might work well. She suggested that she go home to pick up more clothes for herself along with some Disney videos she had for her grandchildren, then go by the grocery store for Gatorade and juice.

At Bob's perplexed frown, she explained, "Gladys Murphy owns the grocery store in town and she's the town gossip. If I swear her to absolute secrecy, the news that Bob has the measles will be all over town within ten minutes after I leave. Small towns know our people." She laughed at the idea of Gladys keeping a secret.

"But won't that scare other people? Measles isn't something to mess with," Bob asked. "I was vaccinated when I was young, but a childhood friend had them and he was really ill."

"Well, those that have been vaccinated won't be scared, and those that haven't been vaccinated will rush down to the clinic to be vaccinated, so they don't get the measles. Win-win," declared the older woman with a beaming smile.

"Then we all know what we have to do. The only thing we haven't considered is that Leeann is bound and determined to leave as soon as possible," Sarah inserted. "Also, Leeann is going to need some clothes, especially underwear and shoes. I can't shop for those for her, it would be too noticeable, and none of my family is her tiny size. Claudia's clothes would wrap around her twice."

"And mine would drag on the ground behind her like a train," piped in Brenna. "She's almost the exact same size as my sister Catherine though. I'll call her, have her pack up some clothes and have someone drop off a box for Leeann at the Spring Hills airport. Then Deke can go pick up the box. Easy-peasy," she laughed. She didn't mention any of the details of exactly how this would be done.

"Make sure that the clothes are real wearable and plain," cautioned Sarah. "Charity isn't gonna' hold well for that girl."

"Catherine probably has clothes she'll never wear, and that still has tags on them. She hates to shop, even online, and considers shopping as a device designed by the devil to eat away people's time. Raina and our Aunt Ulla chooses her clothes and she wears whatever they buy," Brenna explained as Sarah returned to her patient.

Brenna took her phone to the kitchen to make the call although Deke and Bob could hear her as she set it on speakerphone for that purpose.

"Catherine, I think we have a problem, but I'm not sure exactly what one of them is. First, Bob Neal found a woman and two small children in his driveway. She was badly beaten." Brenna went on to tell her all that she knew about Leeann and her situation.

"Then what you need is clothes, shoes, etc.? I have enough clothes for fifteen people and twenty-two elves. Aunt Ulla can't seem to stop herself from her Parisian shopping sprees, and online is too available. And then Raina likes internet shopping too. Ugh. You are more than welcome to everything I have. And yes, I do have some simple styles, probably with the tags still on that we'll remove. We should wash the clothes too, so they don't seem new. Now tell me why your voice sounds as if you're troubled."

"Not troubled exactly, more like uneasy and unsettled which is the second problem." Brenna gave a long sigh. "Catherine, I've never had this happen to me before. When I touch Leeann there is some sort of faint lack of connection. I can close my eyes and run my hands over her like I do with all my patients, but its different. It's altered somehow."

"Explain different. Surely you didn't attempt to bond with

her."

"Of course not. She is not dying." Brenna paused. "It's regarding my other somewhat normal gift. You know that I have healing hands that our long-dead ancestors passed down to a fortunate few. My hands don't see what is inside a person, rather they feel a wrongness when I touch a particular body part that is out of order. With Leeann I can sense a wrongness, but only faintly, like a faraway drum beat. Not like it is typical for me to be able to do."

"And you've never had this before? Ever? Even when you spent all those years with Medical Aid working with a variety of people in other countries?"

"No, never. It seems that I am engaged fully as a physician when the patient is a clan member, or when I'm working with the general public. I've never had someone that doesn't fall into either category. This just doesn't make sense, its kind of scary and frustrating."

"From the little you've told me; I think there are two possibilities that I can think of immediately. The first is that something has changed with you in relationship to Leeann. Or second, Leeann has brought something out in you that is simply new. Neither are necessarily negative happenings."

"I will discuss this with Raina as there may be some long ago association or connection to the past," she added. "As you know, Raina's read every ancestor's journal that we have more than once. She may have a better idea what is happening to you. Or at least she will have some insight. And I would very much like to meet this woman as soon as you feel that she is physically able. In the meantime, I will try to See her."

"Well, it'll be at least ten days before you can come here," laughed Brenna. "That's how long Bob is going to be quarantined for the measles. Call Deke for instructions where to pick up the clothes box."

CHAPTER FOUR

The next couple of days were quiet. Hank used some plastic fence screening for the back patio that could act as a temporary barrier for Sammie and Lizzie. It would allow them to play outside, yet remain in a closed area where they could be watched and not wander off.

Bob had told Lizzie the truth in as simple of terms as he could. Their mother needed to heal and couldn't leave until she was better. And that the Downey's would probably come looking for them.

Lizzie's reaction was typical Lizzie. "I not gonna go. I'm going to hit him with a stick. A big one." It had taken some time to convince her that what she needed to do was to go into her mother's room, and hide behind the clothes in the closet. And she needed to hide Sammy with her.

Finally, they practiced exactly that several times before the children could both run to the second bedroom, through the bathroom, and duck into the walk-in closet behind the clothes. Lizzie said she could be as quiet as a mouse and that Sammie already was.

They all discussed how best to hide Leeann in the event that it became necessary. After reviewing multiple options, it was decided that Leeann, with her slight body, could simply cover herself completely with a sheet. Since Bob was supposed to have the measles, he could lay on the bed and cover himself with a blanket, his back to the door shielding Leeann from view. Sarah would of course stay in the room with her pretend measles patient, Bob.

Hank had taken Leroy Downey's old truck and hid it in the grove of trees a mile or so from the house. The natural camouflage of leafy bushes and overgrown vines made the old truck impossible to view unless standing 5 feet from it.

The problem of what do with the exuberant Hugo was solved with building a large chain link kennel near the chicken coop. With a doggie bed and new bones, keeping him contained would work, at least temporarily.

Hank went into town every day to visit his friends and spread the word that his boss was quarantined with measles. A few old friends laughed, but most of them felt sorry for a grown man to have to go through the childhood disease. Many a story was told of their own bouts of measles. Some of the stories were funny, and some heartbreaking, like the one Joe Collins told of his baby sister dying from the high fevers of the virus. Others were glad that they had been vaccinated young like Hank had been. The more the small town shared their own experiences or non-experiences, the more believable the unusual quarantine became.

On the fourth morning, Hank got a phone call from Police Chief Smyth. "Hey Hank, we can't get in the gate down here. We need to check the area for the Downey's truck. I'm sure you know about searching for Leroy Downey's wife disappearing."

"Sure, Will. I ain't seen hide nor hair of the truck, but I know you've got to do your job. I'll be right down to open the gate as soon as I put the dog in the kennel."

Sarah heard what was happening. She made sure that Leeann was turned facing the wall so that Sarah could cover her body completely with a light sheet. Leeann's slender body made a slight bump in the bed. Sarah reminded her not to move, then returned to her rocker to pick up her knitting basket and an unfinished scarf.

As soon as Bob heard Hank's conversation, he quickly ushered the children into the second bedroom, then on into the closet. Lizzie had stashed a couple of stuffed animals there so she and Sammie would have something to hold. "Lizzie, be very quiet and don't let Sammie move around," Bob cautioned. He hurried back outside to take down the temporary fence, and put the toys in the lidded garbage bin. After a quick check that none of the children's toys or clothes could be seen, he returned to Leeann's bedroom.

He heard a couple of trucks drive up, and Hank telling someone to go ahead and search the barn or sheds, but that there wasn't much to see. The Downey men seemed to hurry off toward the barn, while the police chief and Hank watched them from the porch.

Hugo's bark sounded loud and angry.

Inside, Bob could hear everything that was said. As planned, he took off his shirt, bunched it up tightly to throw in the closet and slid smoothly into bed. He moved close to the sheet-covered Leeann, without touching her. He faced away from the doorway and pulled the light blanket over Leeann and the lower half of his body. He left his large bare back exposed to the door.

"I'd rather have an operation with a butcher knife than do this, Hank," the Police Chief admitted. "I don't know where that gal and those kids are, but I'll bet there was a good reason for them to run and hide. They're going to want to check the house too. Judge Caukins is so frightened of them that he gave them permission, even though it's not legal without individual search warrants."

"Well, they're welcome to search as long as they don't bother my boss. He's had a tough time with those measles. Been real sick. Doctor Ramsey been out here most days and she hired Sarah Hansen to stay with him. It could get real serious I guess."

"I was vaccinated when I was a kid, but my cousin Tommy had them when he was about six. He was so sick we thought he was gonna die. How'd your boss get them anyways?"

"He had to go to New York for business, and thinks he must have got them there. I sure feel sorry for him. Anyway, he's quarantined for people who haven't had them, or haven't been vaccinated."

"We didn't find my truck," Leroy Downey announced spitting on the ground in disgust. "But we'll check the house anyway. Gotta make sure," he stated loudly, glaring at the barking dog in the kennel.

"Sure, boys. Just be real quiet about it. My boss has the measles as you've probably heard. Measles are real contagious. You've all been vaccinated against the measles? Right?" Hank asked.

"Have we?" Leroy asked his brothers, Jake and John, looking back and forth between them. "I don't remember."

Jake scratched his head in thought. "I can't remember being poked by a needle. Can you John? Maybe when we went to school? Or before Ma died?"

At John's frown then negative nod, Hank said, 'Then you've had the measles? You would remember that. They make you really sick with a high fever, cough, and ear infections. Oh and itchy spots all over your body. And the runs. Maybe pneumonia."

The men looked back and forth between each other. "Does that mean we can't go in the house?" Leroy's voice was loud and belligerent.

"Nope," Hank said easily. "If Chief Smyth says you can go over a quarantine, its okay with me. Just be quiet so my boss isn't disturbed. He's has a high fever."

"Hold on, Leroy," advised Jake, the oldest of the group and the leader of the three brothers. "What's a quarantine? What's it mean exactly?"

"Dr. Ramsey said that measles is highly contagious so people can get it easily, and the measles virus gets in the air that you breathe. So people who get near a person who has the measles can get it just by breathing. Or being near them. Even touching whatever they touched," he lied.

The men looked from one to the other.

"Smyth, you go search," Jake demanded.

"Nope. Not gonna' happen. I've got grandkids at home. I don't know if they've been vaccinated or not. I'm not going over

34

a Doctor's quarantine."

Jake's eyes squinted almost closed in thought. "Hank, you open the door and let us look inside without going in. That way we can see if the kids are there."

"Sure, Jake. If you'll wait a minute, I'll even open the bedroom door so you can see Sarah who taking care of the boss. Just be real quiet, please."

The three Downey men crowded into the doorway, looking at the huge room, then on to the open door and the large man in the bed. Sarah didn't move from her rocker, but frowned at the men peeking in the front door.

"That him?" asked Leroy loudly standing in the doorway. "I know that's old Sarah Hansen, the nurse."

"I wanta see," John said, just as noisily, trying to push Leroy aside to get a better view.

"Would you both shut up?" Jake shouted. "I need to think."

Hank shut the door and stood in front of it, sounding exasperated. "He's sick and the Doctor said for him not to be disturbed. If you want to go any further, you're going to have to clear it with Doctor Brenna."

Chief Smyth shook his head in disgust. "Thanks, Hank. They're obviously not here. So Jake, let's move on. Maybe we can get all the way to the Murphy place before dark."

Leroy and John were still arguing and cussing each other when they got back in their truck. Jake got in the driver's seat, made a quick U-turn, and peeled out of the drive. The Chief's car was right behind them.

Hank walked down to the iron gate and locked it before returning to the house. "All clear," he announced in a ringing voice, freeing Hugo.

Bob kept his breathing slow and even, but his heart was pounding. For the first time in five years he had felt a stirring below his belt line. He was appalled with his involuntary reaction to Leeann's cut and bruised body. Thank goodness she was far enough away from him in the bed that she couldn't tell how his body had reacted to her. But being attracted to a married woman in dire straits was not in his makeup.

What the hell was he thinking? The thing was, he wasn't thinking. His body was responding to the nearness of a very appealing female. He carefully moved to the edge of the bed, and stood up, his back to Sarah. "Let me get my shirt and I'll get out of your way," he told Sarah as he entered the walk-in closet. He could hear Leeann ask Sarah if they were gone.

"Is is safe now?" whispered Lizzie from behind the clothes.

"Yeah, you and Sammy can come out now," declared Bob. "They're gone, and you guys were great," he praised. "I even forgot you were in the closet."

The last was the absolute truth. He had been so surprised and horrified by his reaction to Leeann's body that he had temporarily forgotten everything and everyone. Thankfully, everyone else had been so busy that they hadn't noticed his physical reaction.

A jubilant Hank stood at the door. "We did it! They believed us. They won't be back anytime soon. Hallelujah!"

"And you were perfect," praised Bob. "Absolutely believable."

"Can we go out to the back porch to play, Mr. Bob?" Lizzie interrupted. "We gots trucks and we're make'n roads. My dolly, Mary Sue, wants to ride in the back of the green truck. C'mon Sammy, we gots things to do," she asserted as she ran out, Sammie behind her.

That night when Brenna and Deke came over they congregated in the kitchen which seemed to have become the meeting area. Bob and Hank shared their quarantine story and the Downey's reaction. All of them thanked Hank for his quick thinking.

Deke told them that he had decided he would play the good ole boy role when the Downey's came to call. He had been so successful that the Downey's thought he had been born and raised over on Deer Creek instead of the reality in the back streets of Las

Vegas, Nevada.

"Patty, our helper, bragged that Deke's southern accent was so thick she had trouble understanding it. And how the Downey's thought he was one of them before they left," stated Brenna with a giggle.

"That old saying about honey, flies, and vinegar," Deke grinned, folding his six-four self into a small dining room chair. "And Brenna already told me that I couldn't hurt them because it would only bring trouble on us. And maiming them would definitely not be as low profile as Catherine wanted."

"Hey, Dr. Brenna and Deke," Sarah greeted coming into the room. "We have a slight problem. I got a call awhile ago that Benton Phillips is getting out of the hospital on Saturday. You know I'm scheduled to take care of him for a couple of weeks after this last cancer surgery."

"Is it that time already? I've been so busy at the clinic that I had forgotten that we can't keep you forever. When do you have to leave?"

"I'll need to leave the day after tomorrow. Leeann's been up and about, setting in a chair, walking some today and yesterday. I figure by tomorrow I'll have her out here for her meals and to watch TV."

Bob quietly watched the older woman. She had been an enormous help, not only with Leeann but with the children as well. And they were going to need someone to take care of the house and to cook meals. He and Hank had been sharing those duties with Sarah's help, but he was going to need a more permanent solution.

"Sarah, would you happen to know of someone that needs a permanent job that is kind of a cook, housekeeper, and general helper? And that is trustworthy and confidential?"

Before she could answer he turned to Hank and asked, "Do you know someone? I should have asked you first. Would you interview them with me?"

Hank and Sarah glanced at each other and Hank's face reddened.

Sarah grinned. "Would you need this person to live in? Would this more or less be a permanent job?"

"I guess. This idea is about three minutes old, so I don't have much detail of what we need or want. I should have discussed it with Hank first too."

"Yeah, but he would just agree with me," she laughed and winked at Hank. "How about hiring a younger me? I have a sister that was widowed two years ago. No children unfortunately, and her husband didn't leave her well fixed."

Bob knew in the hill vernacular, not well fixed meant that they lived pay-check to pay-check with little to no savings. A hard-scrabble kind of life with more bills than money to pay them.

"Louise does have a nice gentlemen friend that's taken her out several times," she said looking directly at Hank who still had a reddish face. "They've known each other for years so something might come of that," she teased still looking at Hank.

"Ah, ah," stammered Hank. "Louise would be perfect, but I don't know if she's ready to give up her little house."

"Phew," Sarah retorted, waving her hand in dismissal. "That house is falling down around her ears. She fixes one thing and another goes bad. I'm trying to convince her to sell it and get completely out of debt," Sarah asserted sharply.

Hank shook his head, not willing to argue one way or the other in a no-win situation.

"Brenna?" asked Bob, looking for input.

"I know Louise quite well," stated Brenna getting back to the subject, "and she's wonderful with kids. She helped me out some before Patty came. You'd be real lucky if she said yes. Could we table the hiring of anyone for a couple of days though?" she asked. "I'm working on something. And that brings us back to our original question. How can we best help Leeann and the children?"

Everyone was quiet, considering the problem.

"I think it basically it comes to two different approaches, and neither of them are perfect solutions," stated Bob. "We could remove her from the area either temporarily or permanently. Moving her and the children would be easy, but we would leave her with either no support system, or a support system operated by strangers we paid. Money would not be a problem, but I think the added trauma of a new situation might be."

He looked at Brenna as she nodded in agreement. "Or we could suggest to Leeann that she would be better off staying in the area."

"I don't know, Bob. With the Downey men obvious physically abusive, and little to no help from the authorities here, maybe she's be better off out at the ranch in Texas?" she asked looking at Deke. "She would be far enough away that none of them could get to her or the children."

"The ranch hasn't cleared escrow yet," Deke mused, thinking aloud. "We're selling the Texas ranch to our foreman and his family," he explained. "We want to settle here and not run back and forth. I think the Spenser's' would be fine with her and the children staying with them for awhile, but I'm with Bob. That really doesn't solve the problem. It only puts it off. The real problem is what is happening in North Fork and to all the folks who live there. We need a solution that deals with the Downey's and their cohorts. Give me and Bob a couple of days to think about it and talk to some people."

Brenna smiled softly at her pragmatic husband.

"There's no real big hurry now," Bob agreed. "The kids are comfortable here, Leeann is getting better, and the danger is much less. Let's see if we can find a more permanent solution for all of them before we have to uproot them several more times. So let's put off hiring for awhile too."

The group nodded their head in agreement. Sarah went back to her patient and Hank to his small house, leaving Deke, Bob and Brenna alone.

"With a live-in person, how is that going to affect the knowledge of Shadow Valley?" Deke asked. "It will be impossible in the long run for someone like Louise and Hank not to know how special the valley is."

39

"Before we can hire someone from the outside like Louise, we're going to have to talk it over with Catherine. Hank hasn't been a problem because he's known that the Ramsey clan has a large holding on Sky Mountain for his entire lifetime. Maybe Louise has too," she shrugged. "Let's not borrow more trouble than we've already got."

After Deke and Brenna left, Bob remained in the kitchen deep in thought. He had avoided all but the quickest meeting with Leeann, usually just checking her from the doorway if it was open. The children spent a lot of their time taking their toys and playing on the floor of her bedroom. With his own bedroom now upstairs, it was easy to avoid any private time with her at all.

His involuntary physical reaction to her during the Downey men's search made him uneasy and dismayed. How could a man react to a sick battered woman that way? In the years that he had felt free, he had never been attracted to anyone before. Now this injured mass of bruises kept his senses alert and alive. Leeann was married and hurt. And he had to remind himself over and over that it was his job to protect. Period.

CHAPTER FIVE

Leeann lay quietly in bed listening to the gentle snores of the nurse who had been hired to look after her. She had never had anyone care for her needs since her mother died when she was fourteen. It felt odd, out-of-kilter, for someone to be taking care of her. She had no idea how to react to other people paying her attention. Why were all these people helping her? No one did anything for anyone without getting something back.

She could see the edge of one of the twin beds in the next room where the children slept. Every day Lizzie kept an hourly running story of what she did, and the new things she saw. Lizzie told her about the chickens and the dog named Hugo. She heard about all the new food that the children were learning to eat and that they could eat as much as they wanted. Lizzie was fascinated that there was good stuff all the time in a refrigerator. Since Leeann was enthralled with her own introduction to banana pudding, she could understand Lizzie's absorption.

Nothing in her life now was familiar. The room where she slept was nicer than she had ever even dreamed. And everything she saw was clean. Really, really clean. No torn or mended towels. No frayed pillows or blankets. They were all new, or at least looked that way to her inexperienced eye.

There were finely woven sheets and underneath them something Sarah had called mattress pads. The furniture was made of some kind of beautiful wood and polished until it gleamed. The curtains, the comforter, the pillows were all blending colors, much like the beautiful bathroom.

The closet was as large as her entire bedroom had been,

the closet that now held a half dozen beautiful dresses. The dresses were mostly high necked, long sleeved made of pastel cotton print ranging from tiny sprigged flowers to blues and greens muted shades. She had never imagined clothes like that, even in the throw-away magazines that the store owner gave her to use in the outhouse when Leroy didn't buy toilet paper. The white robe Brenna had brought lay across the foot of the bed. It was of shiny white material lined with fuzzy stuff and matched the nightgown she had on. Brenna had said they had belonged to her sister.

The entire experience was one in which she grateful, humiliated, and out-of-place all at once. She couldn't go back to the mountain, Leroy and his brothers would hurt her badly and no telling what would happen to Lizzy and Sammy. And there was no way forward for her to go. No place to belong. Nothing but a large empty void in front of her. She was scared, something that she had been for most of her life. She wanted to be strong, to be in control of her life but that was impossible after she married Leroy. It became even more impossible with Sammie and then Lizzie. She could stand the pain of the physical and verbal abuse much better than her children could have. Standing slowly, she held onto a series of furniture until she went to the bathroom and did her business, moving carefully so as not to wake Sarah. She limped slowly back toward the bed stopping short when she saw a large male standing in the doorway.

"It's okay, Leeann. I was checking to see if the children are asleep," he said just above a whisper. "I don't know how much you remember with all the chaos. My name is Bob Neal. I found you in my driveway, and you're now at my home. Is there anything you need? Anything I can help you with?" he clarified.

"No," she said softly. "I'm sorry if I woke you up. I've slept so much that I'm having trouble sleeping now," she half-smiled. She vaguely remembered this man's voice telling her that she was safe and that everything would be okay. At least she thought that was what she heard.

"Would you like a cup of hot chocolate? I have trouble

sleeping sometimes too, and it seems to help." Before she could answer, he added very softly, "Maybe you'd like to put on a robe and sit by the living room fire for awhile. That contraption in the corner there is a walker for people who have been injured and might fall. Hank, that's my helper and friend, said he used it when he broke his leg a couple winters ago." He walked out, leaving the choice to her.

She carefully fingered the robe before slipping it on, her bare feet peeping out from the floor length garment. She was so sick of lying in bed, maybe it would be all right. She could always call Sarah if she needed help. She cautiously pushed the walking contraption toward the door trying not to disturb the sleeping nurse. The metal walker made moving easier and almost normal. What a wonderful invention.

She sat down in a chair nearest the bedroom and not far from the fireplace, the only source of light in the room. Lizzie had told her that the rock fireplace was big enough for her to stand in and it actually was. The warmth and glow it gave off lit up the comfortable room. The upholstered chair she had chosen was a mix of soft blue, maroon and tans in a muted fabric. The other furniture that she could see was a blend of maroon leather and squishy looking wide armed chairs with square footstools.

"Here you go," Bob said softly moving a tiny table near her chair to set a wooden tray on. The tray held a steaming mug of sweet smelling cocoa with a swirl of whipped cream, at least she thought that's what it was. The tray also held a half dozen or so sugar cookies with cinnamon on top.

Leeann watched from the corner of her eye as Bob took a seat parallel to her, pushed a button on the side of his chair and his feet reclined as part of the chair. She had never seen a chair do that. What a perfect invention. So much new information.

Bob didn't talk but sat quietly sipping from his own chocolate mug, staring into the fire.

"Do you live here by yourself?" Leeann asked softly.

"Yes, there's only me here. And of course, Hank, whom you've met."

Leeann felt herself slowly relax. This was the most comfortable she had been in seemingly forever, at least since her mother died. She didn't realize she had spoken her thoughts of her mother out aloud until Bob asked softly, "When did she die?"

"She died when I was fourteen, I'm twenty-one now, almost twenty-two." She murmured. The warm chocolate and the soft fire light made her feel peaceful and calm. And safe. Here she felt like she was wrapped in a cozy cocoon. She was always on edge when Leroy or his brothers were about as they were completely unpredictable. She never knew what would cause Leroy or one of his brothers to explode into violence. For now, there were no worries either. No worrying about feeding the kids from her limited garden vegetables and summer canning. Or how to ask Leroy to buy salt, baking powder, and other necessities that she needed to cook with.

And her biggest constant fear of all, what would happen to Lizzie and Sammie if she died? If he finally did what he had threatened to do so many times before, make them orphans. Here she was safe. She had made it somehow to shelter, at least a temporary one where she could heal and regroup. She relaxed deeper in her chair.

"I'm 32 going on 82," Bob admitted, his voice a whisper in the quiet room. "Old."

"And probably all the problems I've brought you hasn't made you any younger," Leeann was shocked at the chuckle that came out of her mouth.

"Wouldn't have missed it. I'm glad that I was here to help." Changing the subject to a lighter tone, he said, "And meeting Lizzie and her sidekick, Sammie, has been an experience."

"Even I know that Lizzie is one of a kind. And she's so good with Sammie it's amazing. She's so protective of him. He follows her around like a little duck."

Probing just a little, he said in an idle tone, "Lizzie tells me he isn't her brother, but he's her friend who lives with her."

"Yes," Leeann verified. "Sammie belonged to one of Granny Violet's kin. She raised him when no one else would. When she died, he stayed on with me. He's had a tough time with Leroy." Then repeated truthfully, "We all have, especially since Granny Violet died."

"Your grandmother lived with you? Do you have any other relatives?" Bob wanted to sit up straighter, but didn't dare move and break the tenuous thread of conversation in the dim fire-lit room.

Leeann smiled, still looking only at the fire. "Granny Violet wasn't my grandmother; she was the sister-in-law of my grandmother. She came to live with us a couple of years after they were both widowed. No, I don't have any kin that I know of. I was born on the mountain, so was my mother."

"Death is hard to take no matter what the cause," murmured Bob mostly to himself. They both let the silence stretch out, each thinking back to how death affects others and what the effects had been in their own lives.

Leeann's voice was quiet as she said, "I should have had a baby sister, but she died when I was about five. I would have loved to have had a sister," she said yawning widely.

"I'm so sorry," Bob apologized. "I've kept you up talking when you should be resting. Do you need help getting to your room?"

"No, this walker thing is wonderful, thank you," she said as she walked slowly back to her room to fall into a deep restful sleep.

Leeann woke the next morning to Lizzie leaning over her asking, "You asleep? Don't be, okay?" she coaxed. "Mr. Hank is making those things called whiffles this morning. If you hurry you won't miss them."

"I told you two not to wake your momma up," scolded Sarah lightly from the doorway. "But now that you're awake, Leeann. How do you feel about having breakfast with the children?"

"I'd really like that. Let me get dressed ..."

"No need," Sarah interrupted. "There's just us. No one is going to care if you eat with the kids in your robe." All the time she was talking she was helping Leeann stand, slipping the robe onto her arms, and gently helping her to the bathroom.

After Leeann finished, she washed her hands and run a comb through her hair. There was no way to hide the huge greenish-yellow bruise on her face.

Sarah was right outside the bathroom door and urged her hands toward the nearby walker.

"This walker will help you be more steady on your feet. The more you walk, honey, the stronger you'll get."

Leeann held tightly to the walker. Today she was going to walk as much as she could. She had to be well enough to run again before Leroy and his brothers found her. And he would. She pushed the walker forward and entered the living room with Sarah beside her. They both walked slowly toward Lizzie's voice in the kitchen, followed by a deeper voice.

Leeann stopped in the doorway almost making Sarah plow right over her. The kitchen was magazine worthy with gleaming wooden floors, pecan cabinets, and some sort of shiny gold-colored slick rock on the countertops. The appliances, stove and refrigerator, were black but the other black metal appliance she had never seen the like before. Four stools ran along the center cabinet with a kitchen table that would easily seat ten people near it. Just the kitchen was twice as big as the house she had lived in for the last several years.

I am so out of place here, she thought in a near panic. This isn't my life. She had been so in awe of the kitchen that she had failed to see Bob, Deke, and Dr. Brenna at the table. Hank stood by the stove.

"Join us," urged Brenna. "You're looking so much better."

Leeann blushed scarlet. She was in bed clothes, for heavens sake. When Sarah had said just us, she had taken it to mean just her and the children. She clutched the robe tighter around herself. "I ... I'm sorry," she stammered. "I'm not dressed. I thought ..."

"You're fine," Brenna assured her, plucky at her light sweater. "Actually you probably have on more layers than I do. Please sit here," she indicated the chair across from her. "We came not five minutes ago. I wanted to ask Bob if you had told him anything that would assist us to help you?"

Looking toward the very handsome home owner, she said, "We did talk some. I told him that my mother and I had been born on the mountain." She briefly repeated the conversation to the group.

While she was talking, Hank was busy feeding the children and cutting up their 'whiffles' dripping with sweet smelling warm maple syrup. After they finished eating, he washed their hands and quietly guided them into the living room. He turned on the television to a cartoon channel, returning to stand guard between the kitchen and living room, listening to the others.

"Then you lived with this granny until ...?" Brenna questioned.

"Actually, no. My grandmother and Granny Violet's husbands died. They had married brothers who were killed in a truck accident. My own grandmother moved in with momma and me then. Granny Violet didn't have any kids to help her, she moved in with us after a couple of years had past. My grandmother died, and then my momma died." She took a deep breath, holding her hands together tightly.

"The next week after my momma died, Leroy Downey came and got me, even though I didn't want to go with him. I hardly knew him at all," she murmured. "Granny Violet and him talked outside for a long time, then she told me that I had to go with him." Leeann kept her head down, somehow she felt ashamed of going, but she had had no choice.

"Then what happened?" encouraged Brenna when Leeann's speech slowed.

"We went to see this old man who was the local preacher when he wasn't drunk. He and Leroy talked while I sat outside in the truck, then Leroy came back and said the old man was going to marry us. I was really scared but Leroy said I had to go in. We stood before the old man who mumbled some words that I could barely understand. Leroy gave him some money and we left. We went back to the house and we all lived with Granny Violet until she died a couple of years ago. Then we moved further back into the woods," she said trying to keep everything in chronological order so it would make sense.

It was quiet for several minutes before Deke asked softly, "And you were fourteen years old?"

Leeann nodded her head, not looking up. She had told them the truth. Now they would have to send her back to Leroy because she was married. She belonged to him. Wives belonged to husbands. Granny Violet had said it was in the Bible like that.

"Leeann, was there anyone with you when you married Leroy Downey? Anybody else in the room? Did you have a paper to sign?" asked Deke in his quiet voice.

"No one else was there, just us three. After Lizzie was born I worried about that. I asked Granny Violet about it and she said that Leroy probably had the marriage paper."

"Leeann, I don't want to get this wrong because its important. You were fourteen, and just lost your mother who was your guardian, right?" At Leeann's nod, Brenna continued, "You had no adult with you and you signed no papers? Are you absolutely sure about that?"

Again, Leeann nodded.

"Absolutely sure?" Brenna said, pushing a little.

"Yes, I'm sure. Just me, Leroy, and the old preacher. When I got older I thought about that too. I didn't sign a paper."

Bob couldn't stop the hiss between his teeth. Instead of blurting out his angry thoughts he remained quiet. Brenna and Deke had this under control and had obviously had some knowledge on marriages in Arkansas.

Sarah looked stunned and remained silent, her eyes darting from one to the other.

"I have to be totally honest, Leeann. I'm going to check for records of your marriage, but I seriously doubt I'll find any," Brenna explained keeping her eyes directly on Leeann's. "I'll tell you what I actually do know for sure. Fourteen year olds cannot legally marry in the State of Arkansas. You have to be 18 years old, or you can marry at 16 with your parent's permission."

"I didn't know that. When I asked Granny Violet about it when I got older, she said that it didn't matter anyway because we had lived together so long that Leroy and I had a common law marriage," Leeann repeated, looking miserable.

"I'm never one not to tell the complete truth, and anyway you have to know the rest of it. In Arkansas, there is no such law as a common law marriage. There never has been. Ever."

"Then, then Lizzy...," Leeann felt shattered at the words. Then if Leroy hadn't married her in that old man's ceremony, and there was no common law marriage in Arkansas, she wasn't married? What about Lizzie? What did that make her? An out-of-wedlock child was called a bastard. And it stuck with them forever. They carried it around with them like a sticky shameful brand for their entire life. She couldn't stop the tears dripping off her chin as she swallowed her disbelief and humiliation.

"Stop thinking like that," Bob demanded in his softest voice, seeming to know what trail her mind had gone down. "Children are a gift. Blameless."

Brenna added, "In our culture, there are no words for an out of wedlock child, as there are no concepts for it. Bob and I are a mix of Native American and Scottish as well as other nationalities as are a great number of people. As Bob said, we believe all children are gifts from the Creator. There's an old Native American saying across many tribes that goes for all children no matter under what circumstances. It goes something like 'he's mine as if from my loins. I stole him. I bought him. He was meant to be mine fair'. That's Lizzie. Lizzie has no love for Leroy nor does Sammie I'm sure."

Breann was lost in thought for a moment, then smiled. "In truth, Leeann, this is actually your ticket to freedom and your own life. If it is true, and we all here think it is, as soon as you are healed you are free do do whatever you want to do."

Leeann was breathless. Her life until now was built on a lie? She was silent as she thought though the consequences. And the unknown future.

"I know what you are saying. But you don't understand,

49

none of you do," she lamented quietly, tears slowly running down her cheeks. "I know nothing. Literally nothing. I have little formal education. I only went to school until I was fourteen. I have been taught what Momma and Daddy called the classics that they insisted I learn at home, but I know little else. Simple school stuff like basic arithmetic, reading, and writing of course. Some history. I've never even seen all of the things you take for granted. When I walked into this kitchen I didn't know what most of the shiny appliances were for." She covered her face with her hands as she quietly wept.

Brenna pulled the much shorter woman into her arms. "You're inexperienced, without knowledge of the present happenings, and that can be remedied with time. And adults learn much faster. The things you don't know right now, you can learn. The most important thing is you have friends. Us. All of us," she indicated Deke, Bob, Sarah, and Hank with a sweep of her hand. "And quite frankly, between us all we know a lot," she grinned.

Still sniffing, Leeann answered, "But I'm nothing to you. Any of you. People don't just help other people for nothing in return."

"Sure they do, honey. And so will you once you get on your feet. You'll pass it on, just like we are doing," Sarah inserted. "Other people helped us, and we're all passing it on."

"Whether we were legally married or not, Leroy and his brothers will never quit until they find me," Leeann lowered her head in despair. "His pride would never let him rest. He says he owns me. He will think he's been shamed. And his friends will think so too."

"People can't own people," Bob's voice was strong. "Not only is it against the law, but wars have been fought over that very subject. The Downey brothers need a little education."

Deke and Bob looked at each other in silent communication. First things first, and that was to take care of the Downey men. Scum like that couldn't be allowed to prey on women or men. There was no telling how much pain the three men had caused or would cause if they weren't stopped. And if they were into hard core drugs, they were also probably dealers.

Sarah picked up on the looks between the men and said, "Leeann, first let's get you showered and dressed. Then you'll feel more like yourself. When you're ready you can make some plans. I know that each of us is itchin' to help with those plans. I know I am."

As soon as Leeann and Sarah were out of the room, Deke said, "I gave Kamon a heads up about the Downey's and their friends when I saw him yesterday. He is sure that most of the hard drugs that are peddled in the mountain neighborhoods and the surrounding areas come out of the North Fork community. He also said that the Downey's weren't smart enough to set up a supply chain so someone smarter is involved."

Deke paused before saying, "Bob, since you've had the most involvement with Leeann and the children, Kamon wants to know how you want this played?"

"Played?" asked Hank from the doorway, straightening up sharply.

"Someone has to make the final decisions while Leeann can't. Bob is the logical choice," Deke explained. "Come and join us, Hank. Kamon is our soldier cousin for want of a better word. He knows people that could rid the mountains of the Downey's with little bother or publicity. The Downey's would simply disappear. He was in some sort of semi-government operations for a long time, along with some other stuff," he said with a vague wave of his hand.

"There's another options though. He said we could go the other way which I suggested. Call in some favors with my old bosses at the Drug Enforcement Agency, the DEA, then gather up some old friends in other law enforcement, and go throw the lot of them in prison."

"Cousin or no, Kamon has networking and experiences that are remarkable," admitted Bob, shaking his head.

"True story, and I grew up with him," said Brenna as she grinned, lightening up the conversation and then redirecting it.

"He's mellowed a lot since he married Raina and became a father though. Which means most of the time he's relaxed, easy going and really nice. But there's another warrior side of him that is utterly ruthless."

"He's the father of a couple set of twins," Bob explained to Hank, grinning. "And Brenna is right, he can be rather intense."

"Before you say too much against him, Bob" Brenna teased, "remember how much alike you are. A lot of Kamon's traits and characteristics are also yours. As well as some of your pasts. And that is Raina's truth. And mine."

"Ok Brenna, no more picking on poor Bob," Deke laughed aloud. "We may need all those other qualities from Bob before this is over."

Bob grinned back at Deke, silently admitting the truth in the statement. Many of his own traits and behaviors mirrored Kamon's. He worked hard at tamping down some of his more aggressive, highly focused attributes as he too lived mostly in his own head. He admired the laid-back personality of Deke, but knew that he had a long way to go before attaining that quality for himself.

"Back to the options. What do you think?" questioned Deke.

Shifting his thoughts back to the options that Kamon and Deke had laid out, Bob answered, "You know, I think calling in reinforcements from the DEA and all the others to make a big hoopla out of it would be best. It would be a real deterrent to someone else moving into their little drug kingdom. If that doesn't work, then we still have the second option."

"You can do that? You really can do that? Just call in Big Guns like that? Government folks? DEA and such?" There was awe in Hank's voice and a little bit of horror.

"Just like Sarah said but on a different level. Friends helping friends, and doing what needs getting done. Legally too," Deke's eyes sparkled as he grinned at his gorgeous wife.

"Mas or minus," Brenna laughed fluttering a hand, "more or less."

CHAPTER SIX

The next morning, Bob sat at the table nursing a cup of coffee, thinking about the next few days. Hank had washed up Lizzie and Hank, dressed them in warm clothes and had taken them onto the back porch to play. Hank returned to the kitchen for a second cup of coffee, but seated himself at an angle to watch both children playing their favorite game of dirt, dump trucks, and dolls.

"Hank, I'm so sorry. I didn't mean for you to be stuck taking care of the kids. You're not paid to baby sit."

"There's not enough money in the world to make me do something I don't want to do. Those kids are my reward not my burden, so please let's say no more about it. I should have had some of my own but the army was my wife for a lot of years." Hank frowned in thought. "Aww, Bob I have to tell you something."

He fell silent for several moments, then blurted out, "My grandmother's maiden name was Cameron." At Bob's blank look, he asked, "That doesn't mean anything to you?"

"Should it? I know that Cameron is a Scottish clan."

"Actually, yes it should." Sighing Hank continued, "My long ago ancestors came over after Culloden in the late 1700's with a group of Scots to be resettled here. Long story short, I'm a mix of Irish, Scottish, English, and probably a lot of other nationalities. My daddy's momma was a little Irish lady who might have weighed 110 pounds, was mean as a snake, and smarter than five people had the right to be. She ruled the family, even her adult children. None of us grandkids were taught much about our ancestors, especially our Scottish ones, although a few myths were passed down by pa after his momma died."

He gave a long sigh. "The only way I know anything about my background is my friend, Sarah's sister, Louise, did a DNA test to see if we were related. Thankfully, we aren't," he said, his cheeks turning a faint pink.

Bob held back a grin. Obviously, Louise was special to Hank and in such a close-knit community knowing kinship was important. Especially if things got serious.

"I need to brush up on my history," Bob admitted.

"Do you need me to stick around for awhile? Since Sarah's last day here is tomorrow I thought I'd go into town and check around for awhile."

"No, actually this is a good time. Ask Sarah if there's anything either Leeann or the children need before you go, please."

"Sure, boss," Hank grinned tipping his hat. With one real employee who fell into the friend category, the word boss was a little far-fetched, but Hank liked to tease.

"I was just coming to ask you two if you needed anything from town?" Hank said looking over Bob's head.

"Nothing that I can think of," Sarah said. "Oh, but tell Louise hello for me if you happen to see her," she chuckled.

Bob turned around to ask Leeann if she needed anything. And forgot to breathe.

Leeann stood with her hands on the walker looking uncertain. She was dressed in a dark green dress with fitted long sleeves and a high neckline, a plain dress except that the dress fit Leeann so well it displayed her petite form with all its slight curves. Her facial bruises had faded to a yellowish-green but a cut on her forehead still had a small bandage covering it. The sides of her hair was pulled back into a ponytail on the top of her head, then flowed down her back to join her long hair in a cascade of curls. The dark green dress was the perfect foil for the incredible colors of Leeann's hair; the auburn, blonde, and platinum mix.

She was stunning. Breathtaking.

Hank was having the same reaction, but he had the foresight to say, "You look very nice, Leeann. Your bruises are almost gone."

Sarah beamed as if she was personally responsible for Leeann's beauty. "She cleans up nice," she grinned.

Uneasy, Leeann looked around. "Is there something I can do? I need to work, you've all done so much for me. I can't sit around and do nothing all day. I'll go batty."

Bob's first reaction was to say no, that she needed to rest, but he knew from his own experience that sometimes physical work was a salvation. "Do you feel up to snapping green beans? Hank's garden overflowed and that would be a big help. You can sit at the table here."

"Of course I can do that." Leeann asserted. "And I can peel those potatoes too, there on the counter," she smiled, pointing to the sack of potatoes.

Sarah seated her on one side of the table where she could watch Sammie and Lizzie play through the glass doors. When Leeann sighed in pure joy at being able to help, Bob decided that he had best find something else to do before his body embarrassed him again. She was in good hands with both Sarah and Hank about.

"I have some things I need to do too," Bob murmured, heading toward the door. He hesitated in the hallway. He could go outside to lose himself in hard physical labor of the ranch; there was always work to do. He knew from past experience that tough physical exertion actually alleviated some mental stress. Or he could go upstairs and review some financial records he knew he should check.

Instead his feet took him to the stairway to the second floor and on down the hallway to a door leading up to a third floor. It had been an open attic before he had renovated it months ago. This would be the second time he would see it finished. He took a deep breath, unlocked the door and stepped inside.

Light poured from a glass north wall bathing the entire

open room. The natural light showed off the wide planked floors that had been sanded and re-stained to a dark patina. A small sitting area with a couch and a recliner sat in the far corner. A desk with a computer, large scanner, and a drawing board sat nearby.

Different sizes of blank canvases rested on easels throughout the huge room. Open cabinets along one wall displayed special colored cardboard, stretched canvasses, old jars and containers, and a box of graphite pencils. Paint brushes in holders, sketch pads and several buckets sat beside the double sinks adjoining more cabinets.

Everything was in perfect order as it had been planned. He had supplied the art studio with everything anyone would need to paint.

Three years. Three years since Jennifer had died. Three years since he had painted. At first he had tried to pick up his life after it had come to a stuttering halt. Unfortunately, the lack of feelings for anything lingered, robbing him of emotions. And making him completely unable to put anything on a blank canvas.

He had thought that travel might bring back some significant feelings to his art, so he revisited Europe, with outings to relatives in Scotland. Eventually he had returned to the United States to seek out the dramatic wonders in his own country. Yosemite Valley, then on to the Grand Canyon, then subsequent trips to view the fall leaves in New Hampshire, the spring cherry blossoms in DC, and on to anywhere he thought would help him gain his life back. And the ability to give paint life through the reality of his artist eyes.

Nothing helped. Nothing moved him. Nothing healed inside himself. For part of a year he had even lived in Shadow Valley, the clan holdings at the base of Sky Mountain in the Ozarks of Arkansas.

Art had once been his life's blood. An outlet to express his individual vision and intensity. To represent on paper some of his souls overwhelming strong feelings. With gifted concentration, he had total recall to portray the essence of an individual.

Sometime to portray humor or honesty, but always to catch that fleeting glimpse of reality in a man's face. If he was very luck and patient, he could capture the splendor in the flight of a bird. The goal was always to capture the honesty of that one elusive moment that touched feelings that could never be exactly duplicated.

He removed the covering from the first easel, and picked up a graphite pencil, making two quick lines on the paper. Holding the graphite again was a feeling like coming home – an extension of himself - from his brain's vision to his hand. He moved graphite, letting his mind free.

His eyes were gritty as he finished the sketches. He covered them carefully to preserve whatever he had done. Maybe this could be the beginning of returning to what he had loved all his life. And maybe not. He sat down in a recliner to rest for a moment.

A phone was ringing. Somewhere a phone was ringing. Bob sat upright in the recliner, recognizing that the ringing phone was in his own pocket.

"Hello" he answered, blinking in the bright sunlight and groggy from his art immersion. He had no idea how much time had passed.

"Bob, I wasn't sure where you were, but Deke is here. Says it's important that he talks with you," Hank said hurriedly. "And Sarah is going to have to leave a little early. Her new patient is getting out of the hospital and is clamoring to go home."

"I'll be right there," Bob replied.

No sense in explanations that he couldn't explain and wouldn't even if he could. Hank had not been part of the house renovations, and did not know about the transformation of the attic to a reclusive art studio.

Or that R. Morrison Neal, his artist name, was a famous painter with artwork hanging in people's homes all over the world. And in galleries in New York, London, Rome, and many other large cities.

After locking the art room, he walked down to his room,

grabbed the envelope he had written earlier, and hurried downstairs.

Deke was sitting at the kitchen table with Hank, Sarah, Leeann, Brenna and the children when he entered. Bob thanked Sarah for coming to their rescue making the older woman blush as he handed her the sealed envelope. Sarah tried to hand it back to him explaining that Brenna had already arranged her pay.

"This is a bonus for putting up with all of us," replied Bob sincerely. "You've done so much more, and I wanted you to know how much we appreciate it. I think you're amazing."

The crimson flush spread from her neck to the top of her head. "Ah, ah," she stuttered, "I was just saying goodbye for awhile to everyone. I'm sorry for leaving earlier than planned, but Mr. Phillips needs me, and I promised."

"Okay enough," laughed Brenna stepping in to save her sweetly embarrassed friend. "Sarah is wonderful as she always is, and we're going to miss her. As we decided on the phone, I talked with Sarah's sister, Louise, and she is definitely interested in a housekeeping cum cook job here. Of course, it didn't hurt that Hank is also here," she teased, turning the spotlight on Hank instead of Sarah.

"And glad I am, as my grandfather would say," chuckled Hank, his face tinged with pink. "Ok Sarah, lets head to town. Louise might need my help with a few things."

"Yeah, right," she giggled, dragging the words out. "She just might." She was still laughingly harassing him on their way out.

The children were busy finishing their lunch with a bowl of fruit sprinkled with brown sugar and honey. "We're finished now, mama. Can we be excused? We need to dig up some more dirt for the trucks."

"After you washed your hands, remember? And Lizzie, dry on the towel in the bathroom, not on your sleeve," Leeann told her.

"Okay, mama. Now can we go?" she asked dancing from one foot to the other. At her mother's nod she ran from the room, only waiting at the bathroom door for Sammie to catch up.

Bob had barely glanced at Leeann, now he took a deep breath to ensure that his breathing and voice would be normal.

He could hear Leeann's deep sigh, worry mixed with uncertainty as she stared after her daughter. Lizzie was a handful, probably made worse with newly found freedom after Leroy's abuse and living in constant fear. She was basically a good kid, but with an outsize personality and a mountain of self confidence.

At least with Lizzie around his libido was less noticeable. Her energy and constant movement attracted everyone's attention. He hadn't realized that while he had been watching Leeann, Brenna had been scrutinizing him.

"Bob, Raina called this morning." Brenna said, drawing his attention to her.

"Excuse me, Brenna, I'll see about the children and give you some privacy." Leeann said as she started to rise.

"This is essentially about you, Leeann, please stay." Brenna pulled a note from her pocket. "I wrote down exactly what our little general wanted to know. Raina is the youngest of us three girls," she explained. "She's called the little general because she gives orders like a four star. You'll like her, everyone does. She's married to Kamon Youngblood, whom you may or may not like," she grinned at Bob and Deke who returned the smile. "Kamon is rather different."

"Of course," Leeann answered, "Whatever you want to know. I appreciate all…"

"We are not going there," Brenna stated firmly, emphasizing the not. Glancing down at her paper, she asked. "First, why is your speech and diction not part of the hill community? You talk like a typical educated person, and not at all like Leroy, nor do you have the slang."

"I can talk like that," Leeann chuckled, "but my father and mother made me use good English most of the time. Most of the mountain people who live in the backcountry can talk either way. It's almost like a second language that we can use with outsiders. Letting them know that they don't belong here I guess."

Leeann sighed. "And I definitely have to change Lizzie's speech now that Leroy doesn't yell at her for using good grammar and getting uppity. But to answer your question, my father was the local school teacher. He came there to teach, fell in love with my mother, but he died when I was eight."

"Do you know where he was from? About any of his people? Maybe you have kin folk out there you know nothing about," Brenna said excitedly.

"My mom said that he was an orphan which made her sad because when he died there was no one but us who cared. She said that he came to teach at the little two-room school house because his health was so fragile that he couldn't get hired anywhere else."

"We'll need to talk more about him later, but the next question is if you know anything about the Grannies you talk of. Their names, ages, things like that. Especially about the one that was your biological grandmother."

"Leeann, are you up to this?" interrupted Bob watching her face intently. "It can wait another day or two if you need a delay?"

Bob felt protective toward the tiny woman. She had been through so much. The lack of safety for her and her children from an abusive man, and the fear which must haunt her of not knowing their future. Even knowing that she was more than likely safe from the Downey men's abuse, would not take away the fear from her mind immediately. Only time and continuing security would slowly erase the past.

Leeann smiled softly at Bob. "Thank you, but I want to tell Brenna about me and the past. No one has ever asked me before." Looking straight at Brenna, she smiled. "It feels really good to talk about my mother, my grandmother, and great-grandmother. No one was willing to talk to me about anything much after I married Leroy."

"We'll get to the married part in a few minutes but let's start with your relatives. What was your grandmother's and her sister-in-law's names?"

"My grandmother's married name was Lily Johnson, and her maiden name was Rush. The other granny's name was Violet Johnson; she was my grandmother's sister-in-law. I don't know her maiden name but she was related in some way to the Downey's. They married twins, Gary and Elmer Johnson. Both men died in a truck accident so Granny Violet moved in with us after a couple of years. My mother was Claire Johnson Singer. My father was John Calvin Singer from Tennessee, and my mother said he had no family. He died young, she said he had bad lungs."

Leeann paused to gather herself, then continued in a soft voice. "My mother said she was an only child as her mother had been. My great-grandmother died when I was young, four or five maybe, and her name was Anna Rush. I never thought to ask what her maiden name was, or what my great-grandfather's name was either."

"Most of us don't. By the time we think to ask, most of the old people have passed on. Are there Johnson or Rush cousin's living where you were? Someone you could talk with? Maybe from when you went to school?"

"No. Not that I know of, no one by those names. I went to the country school where my father taught, although Mrs. Sims was my teacher. My father taught older kids. After he died, I went to school until my mother started getting sick. I stayed home to help take care of her before she died when I was fourteen."

She paused momentarily, "Later, after I married Leroy, we lived in the same house with Granny Violet. After she died, we moved out in the woods, away from everyone. I saw a few people when I went to the small store, but most of the time Leroy got whatever I had to have."

Bob shared a quick look with Brenna noting that Leeann had said whatever she had to have, not what she wanted. Had there ever been a time in her life where her wants were met, not just her basic needs? He would bet not since she was fourteen at least.

61

His life had held grief and sadness, but without the gut-wrenching fear that Leeann's life seemed to have been filled with. She seemed to have had no controls over her life and had only felt work and abuse. No protection from anything or anyone.

"Brenna, do you know if I'm married or not? I don't matter, but Lizzie will someday. I don't want her called the names that folks use for those people." Her eyes were shiny with unshed tears.

Deke answered her question. "Leeann, I was in law enforcement for a lot of years. I also studied law for awhile." He took a deep breath, "I looked for any certification of marriage everywhere there is to look. Finally, I called an FBI friend of mine who's a computer geek to be sure I had as much information as possible."

Holding her gaze, he said quietly, "No. You are not married. Leroy ran a scam on you, and people were so frightened of all the brother's brutality that they didn't question whatever he said."

"No one dared go against them," Leeann agreed, her lips trembling. "They would have gone after their families in the cruelest way possible." Turning back to Deke she asked, "Does that mean that I don't have to do whatever he says? That I don't have to go back if he finds me? That I can leave the area if I want?"

"That's exactly what it means." Deke broke out in a wide smile, "Leeann, you're free to do whatever you want to do. Go, stay, whatever."

"For real?" she asked wide-eyed, wiping the tears drying on her cheeks. "It all sounds wonderful, except the part about Lizzie."

"Yep," Deke answered beaming. "It's for real. Honest."

The truth seemed to be dawning on Leeann if the huge grin beginning to spread across her face was any indication.

Bob had felt his heart turn over when she talked about leaving the area. He had just met her yet felt connected to her and her children in a way he had never felt before. He wanted to explore the possibilities. To see if there was a glimmer of life left inside his shell of a body. To see if he could have a love again. For that he needed time.

Keeping his thoughts hidden, he stated calmly, "That's wonderful news, Leeann. First you'll need to be completely heal though. Right, Brenna?"

Brenna gave him a narrow eyed stare, the what-are-you-up-to kind before she said slowly, "Yes, you do need to be completely well before you decide to take on the world. You don't need a nurse anymore, but you do need to gain your strength back. You also need to learn a few basic skills and information before you decide to conquer this part of Arkansas," she smiled to take the sting out of her blunt words.

Leeann's glance took all of them in. "I know so few things that truthfully I don't even know where to start. But first I think I need to feel safe from Leroy. Even if I'm not legally married to him, he will make me do whatever he wants me to do. He'll take Lizzie away from me. I'll do whatever he says to keep her and Sammie safe," she admitted softly.

"Nope," Bob said with steel in his voice. "He won't. We can protect you here. Hank and I will always be here until law enforcement decides when they plan their drug bust, or whatever they decide to do. Hank and I had some fun target practicing last summer and we're both good shots. Deke?" he grinned.

He knew that all three men were better than good shots. With Hanks military training, Deke's law enforcement plus both of their Warrior training, they were much, much better than good. He had asked the question only so that Leeann knew they had the ability to protect her.

"As am I," Deke agreed. "We'll also set up a more extensive security system here just in case the Downey's have some nasty friends. We'll know if anyone steps foot on the property near the house."

"I should leave. This is too much trouble for you all," groaned Leeann. "You've already done so much for me and my kids."

"Truthfully, we really haven't. So far it's been kind of fun," Bob chuckled. "This house was much too quite before Lizzie and Sammie came. Well, Lizzie at least," he laughed, thinking of the silent Sammie.

"Speaking of Sammie, do you know why he doesn't talk?" asked Brenna. "Is there something wrong with his vocal cords, like a birth injury?"

"I don't know for sure, but I remember that Granny Violet said that he couldn't make any sounds and that's why he couldn't talk."

"He can't make any sounds? Do you mind if I examine him the next time I'm over here? I can't do it today, but in the next couple of days?"

"Sure, he's such a good little soul," Leeann stated warmly. "He's never any trouble."

"Hmmm," Brenna replied her eyes thoughtful. "Ok Deke, let's head out. You promised Brandon that he could ride with you today. He's probably standing by the door waiting." They shared a deep private smile.

CHAPTER SEVEN

Bob sat quietly, thinking about the relationship between Deke and Brenna. He had been told that their courtship had been rocky and turbulent. His auburn-haired cousin had a temper equal to her beauty, and her unusual abilities led to a strong personality. He had been told that Deke had issues left over from his time in law enforcement. and was a loner before he met Brenna.

Somehow they had fused into a solid family unit, and he was green with envy. He wanted what they had. That special sharing, the connection that no matter what else came in living life, another person would always be there by his side. The give and take of every day life. Sharing thoughts and making dreams together. Something he had lost before it was fully developed. Or maybe could never have been.

"I'd better check on the children, see if they need anything," Leeann said.

"Sure," Bob said casually. He knew she could see the two kids playing on the back porch from where she sat, so she must need an excuse to leave. "Louise, Sarah's sister, should be here in a couple of hours. You may be more comfortable then."

"Actually, I'm not uncomfortable. I've never been around many men but you don't make me nervous. I thought you might like some privacy. I've been nothing but trouble for you since I came here".

"You really haven't been," Bob denied honestly. "After the house was remodeled and furnished, I wasn't sure what to do with myself. Having you, Lizzie, and Sammie here has made everything better. I enjoy all of your company. Honestly, I hope you choose to stay here for a long time."

"Choose ... I get to choose," she murmured, softly smiling to herself. "I get to choose," she repeated, her smile reaching her sparkling eyes.

"Mr. Bob. Mr. Bob, hurry there's a puppy by the barn," Lizzie yelled. "Hugo is sniffing him. Will he hurt him? Can we go see?"

"Wait right there for me, Lizzie. We'll go together. Do you want to come Leeann? I'll be sure it's safe before the kids go down there."

Standing up immediately, Leeann nodded. "I would. The kids might need me."

The puppy turned out to be a mid-size adult female dog in the first stage of giving birth. Hugo seemed to be standing guard over her in a protective stance.

"Well, well. Aren't you a pretty little girl," Bob stage whispered, allowing his hand to be sniffed by the little female dog. To the watching group he explained, "Someone probably dropped her off to fend for herself before she has this litter of puppies. Let's see if we can't get her into the garage and make her a little more comfortable. The garage is heated and there's a sink out there." Bob gently picked up the female dog carrying her toward the house while the others trooped behind him. Hugo following closely.

"Leeann, there's an old blanket and a large wicker laundry basket just off the kitchen in the utility room. Could you get that, please. Lizzie, can you get that metal pan over there, fill it half full of water, and bring it here. This little lady may be thirsty." Everyone quickly completed their chores. Hugo and Sammie stood side by side watching the others, Sammie's small hand resting on Hugo's back.

"Leeann, she's going to whelp very soon, I would guess in the next hour." He was silently telling her that if she didn't want the children to see a live animal birth, she needed to take them in the house.

Leeann seemed undecided for a moment, then said, "This is a ranch, and seeing a live birth is part of learning. May we all stay? We'll be real quiet, okay Lizzie? Sammie?"

Forty minutes later, the female dog delivered the first black and white puppy to soft gasps of awe from the four bystanders. Two reddish-brown puppies followed. The mother licked the tiny blind puppies clean, and they rooted around until they found a teat for their first meal. The female dog lay quietly in the basket, her eyes closed in exhaustion.

"Wow," Leeann exclaimed, "That was incredible. And the puppies are so cute, even all wet," she enthused. "Oh look, here comes Hank and another car."

Lizzie immediately ran to Hank telling him about the 'drop-off dog' and her puppies, and that having the puppies was messy and the puppies were blind but their eyes would open soon and on and on before she had to take a breath. Only after her explanations were finished did Lizzy pull Hank over to look at the newborns, where he gave the appropriate oohs and ahhs.

"Those are fine looking puppies," he announced, "prettiest ones I've seen for awhile.
Louise, this is Bob, our boss, and Leeann, a guest. And Lizzy and Sammie," he smiled warmly at the pretty woman who exited the car.

Louise shook Bob and Leeann's hands and smiled at the two small children. Louise turned out to look like a smaller forty-ish year old versions of Nurse Sarah. Her blond hair was lightly streaked with gray, and her smile was wide and warm like her sister's.

Noting several boxes in the back of Hank's truck, Bob suggested to Louise, "Let's go in and help you get settled first, then Hank and I can bring in your stuff. Welcome to your new home, Louise. Thank you for coming to help us out. I hope you'll be happy here."

"Can we stay out here? Please. Please," Lizzie begged, interrupting. "We won't touch the mama dog or the puppies, we promise. We just want to watch them for a few more minutes."

Leeann lifted an eyebrow at Bob, silently asking his permission. At his nod, she said firmly, "Okay, but remember what a promise is. That's your word. Your good name."

"How about I put a couple of lawn chairs right here for you two to sit in so you're comfortable? When you get off the chairs, you have to come in the house." Bob set two chairs several feet away from the new momma, well out of touching distance. Both children hurriedly climbed into them, their feet dangling.

Leeann followed Bob into the kitchen area to see if she could help, and to become acquainted with the other woman. While the men brought in several suitcases and a couple of boxes, Leeann asked Louise what she could do to help.

"I'm so glad to be here," Louise confided. "That apartment back there is about the nicest thing I've ever lived in, it even has an outside entrance," she said, not meeting Leeann's eyes. She bustled around the kitchen, looking in cabinets and checking the supplies. "Do you think you could put away my kitchen knives and some of my favorite pans? Nothing heavy, mind you. Hank said you've been ill."

Been ill. Well that was one way of looking at it, Leeann thought ruefully.

"It's going to be so much fun to cook in this kitchen," Louise gushed. "All the appliances are first rate and the pantry is full of supplies. It looks like there's everything a woman could want. Now, is there anything that the children won't eat. Or that they really hate?"

Leeann laughed out loud. "Honestly Louise, in my world, if it was food, whatever it was, we ate it and was grateful to get it. The kids are not picky at all. Of course, their favorite thing to eat is something sweet, and since I've tasted banana pudding, I can't blame them," she chuckled.

When Bob and Hank walked in with the last boxes to be unloaded, the women were naming the foods that the kids might love. Bob looked from one woman to the other one then back again. "Ah Hank, lets go out and do the ranch chores, they don't seem to need us right now. Leeann, we'll watch Lizzie and Sammie. That is if we can tear them away from the new puppies."

The women barely nodded as they continued to talk. Bob

shook his head smiling. Leeann looked like she had found a long-lost friend, someone female she could talk with.

A couple hours later, Bob, Hank and the two now sweaty children stomped into the house laughing about Hugo and his new companion.

"Mama, mama" Lizzie said excitedly, "Mr. Bob says that Hugo thinks he's those puppy's daddy. He is laying down out there right beside that 'drop off' dog. And that dog don't gots a name. Can we name her, momma? Please."

Leeann laughed as she shared a quick grin with Bob and Hank. "We'll have to talk about that later. Names are important. Okay Lizzie and Sammie, get washed up for dinner." Both kids immediately ran to the bathroom followed by the men.

Leeann was wearing a frilly apron which obviously be-longed to Louise. The two women seemed to have bonded in the short time the men had been outside. Now they shared bringing the bowls of food to the table.

Noting Bob's frown, Hank murmured so only he could hear. "Louise needs to be needed. She has a really sweet nature about her. She should have had a houseful of kids and grandkids. She'll help Leeann learn things she should know. It'll be good for the both of them."

"Hank, how in the hell do I ever repay you for all you do? You bring so much to this little family and to me. Now, to Louise, and others in the community."

Hank grinned and bumped his shoulder to Bob's. "My life is all good. And it may get better," he said real loud, as he winked at Louise.

Louise blushed and turned away, doing her best to ignore her reddened cheeks and the men. Neither Bob or Leeann said a word but the grins couldn't be hidden.

That evening Deke and Brenna came over with Brandon, their three-year-old. Lizzie promptly took him to the garage to show off the new puppies as if she was the tour guide.

"Now mama, don't worry. We won't touch the puppies, and Brandon will not touch them neither," Lizzie assured the group of adults. "Mr. Bob says they're too new to be touched, so I won't let anyone do that," she asserted strongly, glaring at the two boys as they followed her out the door.

"Are you sure she's only four years old?" asked Deke, with laughter in his voice.

"I'm sorry," sighed Leeann. "She's always been bossy. Now she seems to think that she is the boss of anyone under 10, but would love to boss the whole world, starting with me."

"It'll help when she goes to school," Brenna assured her. "It must have been hard for her to have no other kids to play with except Sammy who doesn't talk back to her. Kids learn from each other how to socialize. She'll find other kids like her in school. Now to you, any pain twinges for you, Leeann?"

"No I actually feel fine. Louise made me sat down, it's the only way she allowed me to help her."

School. Lizzie and school. Where would they be? And Sammie? How could she take care of him when she was working. With her very limited knowledge and experience, could she even keep food in their mouths and a roof over their heads? She forced herself back to the conversation.

"Bob, I know that you and Hank have already talked to Louise about confidentiality as have I, so we're going to skip to the good stuff. Your ten-day measles quarantine will be up Tuesday. Deke, it's yours," she indicated the floor with a sweeping flourish of her hand.

Deke grinned broadly at his vivacious wife, "So," he continued his wife's sentence, "next Tuesday is the day that the DEA is planning its raid. It's turned out easier than any of us thought. The man the Downey's kicked to death was a young man whose uncle is an Arkansas State Senator. He's raised all kinds of hell for an investigation and he's going to get one."

"Law enforcement will be gathering just after the turnoff on road 204 before dawn. They plan their raid just after dawn when most people will be asleep. There's a slew of people coming, FBI, DEA, Sheriff Department, State Police, and some high-powered SWAT teams."

"Road 204? Deke, that's where the Lukens live, and the little marijuana grow community is," she reminded, frowning in consternation.

"No worries, Brenna. I introduced Sam Lukens to the DEA supervisor so we could ask him for help in keeping that road clear. We don't want innocents hurt," a pain flashed across his face. Brenna placed her hand on his arm. "Sam will see that the little community hunkers down during the time of the drug raid. With their guns handy of course," he grinned, thinking back to Sam and his little community of hippie dropouts.

"Whew. Thanks, there's some good people out there. And some not-so-good ones too," breathed Brenna. "They may get better after the raid with the drugs gone," she grinned, sharing a glance with Deke.

"Leeann, would it be all right if I come over after breakfast in the morning to examine Sammy. I'd like to see the cause of why he doesn't talk. It could be a birth defect, or an injury during birth. It could also be something as simple as a speech delay. He seems to understand everything that's going on around him."

"He does," agreed Leeann. "My problem is I've never had anyone to talk with to see if I could help him. Leroy always wanted him out of his sight. And Sammy hid when Leroy was about. Most of the time Lizzy hid too."

The group remained silent. There was nothing to say about a man that would pick on a defenseless, disabled child. Or maybe too much to say.

Brenna arrived after breakfast the next morning, a small black bag in her hand.

"Physicians tools," she explained to Hank as when he opened the door. "I'd like for both Lizzie and Sammie to be here," she requested, taking a stethoscope. There's other things here but I think I'll use ...," her voice drifted off. "Other ways," she amended, glancing at Bob.

"I'll get the kids. They're out seeing how the mama dog and her puppies are this morning."

"Those puppies are a major attraction. Brandon is begging

71

to come back over to play," Brenna said, moving out of the way as the children rushed back to the house.

Lizzie slid to a stop in front of Brenna. "Mama said you wanted to examine us? Why? What'ca looking for? Do we gots something?" she asked worriedly.

"Nope," answered Brenna in a casual tone. "Today, I just want to check if you're okay. You do know you go to school in the fall, right?"

"Yep, and I'm going to be so good. Mama says I will love school and mama don't lie."

"Mamas don't," agreed Brenna. "Ok Lizzie, you first. I want you to stand in front of me. Yes, just like that," Brenna said, as the little girl stood up straight in front of her. "This is a stethoscope I use to hear things inside you. First I will hear your heart beats, then you can hear mine." She inserted the ear pieces into her ears and heard Lizzy's normal heart beat of a child. She carefully inserted the ear pieces and watched the awe on Lizzy's face as she listened to Brenna's heart.

Brenna went through the same procedure with Sammie. She drew a sharp breath when she heard the uneven rhythm of Sammie's heart beats. She closed her eyes to concentrate fully. Turning so that her back was to Leeann and Bob, she took the stethoscope out of her ears and moved her hands carefully over Sammie's chest.

She knew that fifty percent of Down Syndrome children were born with congenital heart defects. Many of the physical signs of Tetralogy of Fallot were visible for Sammie, a term given to a heart condition composed of four abnormalities. Also she sensed the most common heart defect for Down Syndrome children, AVSD, atrio-ventricular septal defect. Surgery before age five could have helped both conditions immensely.

Hiding her own dismay, Brenna smiled at Sammie and continued to carefully move her hands over his low set ears, across his chest and to his throat. Her hands paused over his throat for several minutes before moving on. "Sammie, you are wonderful," she declared, giving him a hug.

Lizzie beamed as if she was personally responsible for his well- being, which in some ways she had been. Leeann had said that Lizzie had been with him since she was born. She had evidently assumed the big sister role and had taken it seriously, teaching and role modeling as only a peer could.

"Okay guys, you can go back to the puppies now. You two are good for school, Lizzie."

"Yeah, let's go see if that black puppy gots out of the box yet," instructed Lizzie running to the door. Sammie followed more slowly but as fast as he was able.

Bob waited until after the children had shut the door. "Brenna?" he asked softly. "What's going on?"

Instead of answering Bob, Brenna asked Leeann, "How much do you know about Sammie's Down Syndrome?"

"A little," responded Leeann slowly. "Grandma Violet wouldn't talk about it at all, but I read about it in my school dictionary. I know there is no known cause and it's a chromosome disorder. And that older mothers have more Down Syndrome children. Grandma Violet would not tell me who the mother of Sammie was, so I have no idea how old his mother was either."

"Then when this Grandma Violet died, you just kept Sammie? None of her family came forward?"

"Humph, her family was Leroy's family too. They were a bunch of never-do-wells. I kept him because there was no one else to care for him. Besides, I love the little guy, so does Lizzie."

"Unfortunately, he has a host of medical problems, Leeann. And damn, I hate this part of healing." She paused to gather her thoughts. "Besides his being at higher risk for a multitude of health problems from AVSD, the most common heart defect for a Down's Syndrome child, he also has a heart condition known as Tetralogy of Fallot. It's a term used for a heart condition composed of four abnormalities. His lungs are not developed as fully as they should be either, so the blood flow to the lungs is limited. And he has some other problems."

"Is there anything that can be done to help him?" asked Bob quickly, giving Leeann a chance to absorb the new information.

"Unfortunately not a whole lot. If he had been diagnosed earlier, especially in the first year of life, surgery would have helped. Without going into a lot of medical terminology, I have to tell you that his medical problems are extensive. More than likely his physical health will decline as he gets older."

Leeann's hands covered her face, "No, not Sammie. No."

"I seem to always be the carrier of bad news, but in order to take as good care of Sammie as possible, all of us must deal with reality. Knowing the truth will help do that."

Wiping her tears, Leeann admitted, "I have seen some changes in Sammie in the last year. He sleeps more, his fingernails are slightly blue, and he is clumsier. Is that part of his medical problems with Down Syndrome?"

"Yes, and there's more. I wanted to check why he doesn't talk. There are two reasons. His mental and physical development are retarded, slower to develop, which is not truly abnormal with his disability. But there was a windpipe injury either during birth or immediately afterward."

Leeann thought back to all the tiny snippets of information that Grandma Violet had said about Sammie. No one wanted him. They did not want to claim him. He was a secret that some people needed to keep. Had someone tried to harm him as a baby? Was that why Grandma Violet lived with them? Was Sammie connected to the Downey's and to Grandma Violet somehow? With so many dead, the truth might never be known.

"I love that child," Leeann said firmly. "He's mine. What can I do to help him?"

"You're doing it," declared Brenna truthfully. "He's amazingly stable. He's not fussy, nor aggressive. He will have continuing health problems, and I will monitor them. I won't give you a list as it might be confusing."

"If you feel you need to know more, as soon as you can use the computer you can look up anything or you can ask me anything. But Leeann, I will give him the best care that is possible for anyone to have."

Brenna paused to be sure Leeann understood. "And he may live a long fruitful life, or he may not. Much like the rest of us."

CHAPTER EIGHT

The following Tuesday Bob was up before dawn to make coffee, which he discovered had already been made. He poured himself a cup and took it to the front porch expecting to join Hank. Instead, Leeann sat sipping a cup of coffee, staring into space.

"Couldn't sleep?" Bob kept his voice low and slow, not wanting to disturb her. Or himself.

Leeann glanced at Bob. He was the most beautiful man she had ever seen, and the nicest one too. "Yeah, I've been up for awhile. I just have so many mixed up emotions. This morning is the raid on North Fork. Maybe the little community will survive or maybe not."

She shrugged, giving a deep sigh. "I feel sorry for some of the people who will be caught in the raid. Many of them are drug addicts and need help, not jail. Then there's those like Leroy, Jake, John and their friends who have threatened and terrorized everyone. I have trouble feeling sorry for them. A few people were kind to me, at least as much as they could be without risking the Downey's backlash."

"It will be over pretty soon," Bob said softly reminding himself that she was here temporarily, not permanently. Much as he had enjoyed her company she would leave as soon as she learned more about life, and realized the options in front of her.

"I want ... I want," Leeann stopped, then started again. "It's hard for me to wrap my head around that I'm probably a single woman with two kids. That I was never married. It was what Louise called a scam where I had no choice." She gave a long sigh.

"I can't remember when I had a choice in what I wanted to do. Mama told me what I should do because I was a child, then after she died, Leroy made me do whatever he wanted me to do. Even Granny Violet gave me orders."

She rubbed a hand across her face, "I've talked a lot to Louise in the last couple of days. If I really do have a choice, I think what I want is to be normal, like I think other people are. I want to work, take care of Lizzie and Sammie, go grocery shopping, maybe even to that McDonalds that everyone seems to know."

Bob grinned at her simple requests and remained silent.

"And I want to learn. I want to learn all the things I've missed. It may take awhile because I know nothing," she laughed, poking fun at herself. "Louise says that she'll teach me the basics of the computer, and that there's schools you can go to on it. Like a real school with teachers and stuff. Isn't that amazing?" she said, wonder in her voice. "A person can learn anything on the computer Louise said. For me, that little box screen is magic. I've barely seen a television." She grinned ruefully.

"You might like to start with some documentaries on television. There's a documentary for everything anyone has ever done, or thought, or fought. Some are strange or funny, but most of them are educational, and all of them are informative in one way or another."

Leeann had told Bob that her grandmother, then her mother and teacher father, had taken turns reading the classics to her aloud. Leeann knew the writings from Shakespeare to Mark Twain, but hadn't a clue how to use a modern dishwasher or an electrical appliance. She seemed to have a good grasp of ancient history and no knowledge whatsoever of what had happened in the world since she was fourteen. Her crisis year.

Since the death of her mother, and subsequent fictitious marriage to Leroy Downey, he suspected she had been in survival mode.

To check if his guess was correct he asked, "Then you didn't go to school at all after your mom died?

"No, I wasn't even allowed to read unless I was alone. I hid my books so I would at least have some familiar friends." She closed her eyes with a sigh. "Leroy told me what to do and when to do it. Granny Violet went along with him. I was such a coward and I had nowhere else to go. I don't have proper words to explain, but I just got through every day as best as I could with no plans for the tomorrows. Tomorrow was something I didn't think about. It was hard enough just getting through every day."

She didn't look at him. "I didn't have any say about anything. Not when I could sleep, or what I should cook, or talk to anyone but the Downey's or Granny Violet. I didn't go to church or anywhere else because Leroy said I couldn't. He didn't tell me why, he just said no."

"At first, I thought it would get better with time, but after Lizzie was born, it got worse. The Downey brothers told me how ugly and worthless I was because I couldn't give Leroy a boy baby. And I didn't get pregnant again. They said that I couldn't cook food worth eating, and on and on. After Granny Violet died, it got really bad. She left me Sammie to care for, and Leroy moved us to a little house further into the woods." Tears ran unchecked down her cheeks. "And Bob, I never want to talk about this again, okay?"

"Done." Agreed Bob. He had heard it once and it broke his heart. He did not want to hear it again either. "From now on, let's talk about what you want, or what you need for you, Lizzie and Sammie.

Leeann gave a quick grunt, "Need? Truthfully, I don't know what I need, it's all too new to me. I know I need to get a job to work and support us. But what I want is to know stuff, maybe even go to school."

Bob didn't dare tell her she was almost non-hirable with no formal education, no network to help get a job, or childcare for the children. She had worked hard her entire life and had made 'doing without' a mantra. "Is there any particular subject you want to study? Or just general education?"

"I want to know a lot of things. Everything actually. Do you promise not to laugh if I tell you what I would like to know more about?"

At his solemn nod, she continued. "I like to sew, to make quilts for the beds, or for hanging on the wall. My mind sees color everywhere. I love blending fabric colors so I want to study that, if there is such a thing. Louise thinks it's called textile design, and you can study it on that internet box."

Of all the things he had been expecting that would have been his very last guess. Art. She wanted to study a form of art. His heart pounded and his mind went to crazy places. He could teach her. Everything she ever wanted to know, and he had the contacts for her to sell her fabric paintings if she wished. He could …. He stopped himself. First he needed to know if he could even help her in the small things, if she was willing to let him help. And he would have to go very, very slow as Leeann was very vulnerable.

"Hmmm. Do you get along well with Louise?" asked Bob, casually keeping his voice nonchalant.

"Of course, I do. She's a wonderful person, she reminds me of my mother."

"Then maybe we could solve each other's problem." He hesitated for several moments to give her a chance to consider that he had a problem too.

"This house is too big for Louise to handle cooking, cleaning and everything else, so Hank and I thought we'd hire another person." He reminded himself to tell Hank about the discussion that wasn't.

"Would you be interested in a housekeeping job until you get on your feet? Know more of what you want to do?" he shrugged as if indifferent to her answer. "That way Louise could also help you learn a little about the computer in your spare time. There's room and the children seem to like it here."

"Really?" asked Leeann, her eyes sparkling. "Oh, but you're right. The house is too big for one person to keep up. And the cooking and everything else. Oh Bob, that would be wonderful. I could learn a bunch of stuff that I need to know. And you do need someone else to help Louise. It wouldn't be like I was taking charity. I'll work hard, I promise. I'm glad that's there's a job for me," she beamed. "I've got to go tell Louise," she laughed excitedly, rushing into the house.

Bob remained sitting on the porch, taking up Leeann's role of staring into space. He had time. And maybe so did she.

Brenna was the only one who came over that evening. A quiet, solemn Brenna looking as if she would rather be anywhere else in the universe except with them.

"Bob, would you gather everyone into the kitchen? Maybe put on a kid's video for Lizzie and Sammie please."

Bob quickly complied, letting the children watch Lady and the Tramp for the upteenth time. The rest of them, Leeann, Hank and Louise, gathered around their meeting spot, the kitchen table.

Brenna addressed Leeann first. "You know the law enforcement raid took place at dawn. There were dozens of agencies there. Deke went as a local observer, more to keep a few people out of the law enforcement net than anything else. He's still with them, but he asked me to come and tell you what happened before the information spreads. There were several people killed during the conflict."

She took a deep breath and let it out slowly. "Leroy and John Downey were two of the fatalities, the other two were Doug Olson and James Melon. There are eight wounded, including a Sheriff's deputy. Two of the wounded are critical, Jake Downey is one of those. I don't know how many were arrested." Her voice stopped as she waited for Leeann's reaction.

"Do you know what happened?" Leeann asked softly with her head down, her hair shielding part of her face.

"Deke said several men were holed up in a house, and refused to surrender. Instead, they made the decision to shoot it out with law enforcement. Suicide by cop, or maybe just drugged up and making poor decisions. Doug Olson and James Melon were in the same house as Jake Downey and a couple of others who were wounded." She waited a couple of moments, then added, "I'm sorry, Leeann"

"I am too," came the soft reply. "He was Lizzie's father even though he was a terrible one. Would you excuse me, please?" she asked going into her bedroom and closing the door.

A couple of minutes later, Lizzie rushed into the room, her hand on her hips. "Who did it? Who made my momma cry?" she yelled angrily, while Sammie stood staring at the group.

Brenna knelt before Lizzie, holding her gaze. "I had to bring you momma bad news," she admitted quietly. "Your dad died this afternoon." She didn't give any details and didn't use the word killed.

"He's dead? Forever dead?" Lizzie questioned, eyes wide. "You're sure?"

At Brenna positive nod, Lizzie chewed on her lip for a moment, then turned and fled into the bedroom where her mother had gone, Sammie following more slowly.

"Now, I think I need to go home and hug my children," Brenna said, leaving the kitchen. "If there's any other news, I'll either come over or call you," she said to the group. "This day has been a hundred hours long. The wounded were brought into the hospital where guards have been stationed. It's chaos. I helped as much as I could," she grimaced, then walked out.

"If either of you need me, I'll be in the library. It looks like Leeann has put the kids to bed so I'll say goodnight," Bob said. He could hear Louise ask Hank if he wanted more coffee as he left the room.

Instead of going to the home library, Bob walked slowly up to the third story of the house, absorbed in the sharp contrast between his and Leeann's pasts.

He had been born to older parents who had been caring, doting but not smothering. They had been killed in an automobile accident when he was in college. He still missed them and their quiet way of giving advice only when asked. Maybe he wouldn't have made so many mistakes if they had been there.

Since early childhood he had been admired for his unusual good looks and striking coloring. His mother had said that people had stopped her on the street to tell her that he was pretty

81

enough to be a girl. From his earliest memories he had shied away from the admiration. As he got older, his body grew into a large physical stature much like his father's, sculpturing the prettiness of his face.

As an only child he was naturally a loner. Only after discovering his artistic ability could he reconcile the dichotomy of his own being. With paint he could express the intense feelings that rushed through his body. Art was his outlet.

Even when he was in middle school, when other boys had been up to bat at the baseball diamond, he had been sitting in the dugout doodling on a slip of wrinkled paper, or sketching in the dirt with a stick. He had been teased, but thankfully he was big enough, and a good enough athlete, that the teasing wasn't too intense.

Later, in high school, his educational focus had been art, but he had a few close friends, and even a few friends that were girls. There had been no special girl though. He had been uneasy about whether they actually liked who he was as a person, were attracted to his outer appearance, or to the challenge that he seldom dated.

And his summers were not as carefree as his peers. He and his parents lived on an elderly uncle's cattle ranch near the reservation. As in many Native American households, there was a free-flow of visiting relatives to the ranch during the summers. Any relative was welcome for a day or an extended time. The elderly uncle's only rule was that everyone contributed in some way, in whatever way they could. His mother had enforced that rule and trouble-makers were thrown out with the help of a multitude of cousin helpers.

He had always thought that he had the best of both worlds, art during three seasons of the year, and heavy physical outdoor work during each summer. He loved both.

After his parent's death, there was a sizable trust fund that he had not been prepared to handle, nor anyone to limit any accesses he sought from his grief. Like a new drunkard, he had indulged himself in alcohol, sex, and art until he had almost flunked out of all his college classes.

That was the summer that Grandfather Youngblood came, got him and set him his feet on a different path. That summer he spent in the Highlands of Scotland in the school for warriors, the Swords and Shields.

Grandfather Youngblood had told him his artistic gift was to see and portray Truth, but his destiny was to Protect. And that it was a lifetime commitment.

He returned to school after that summer stronger in body and in mind. He hired a tutor, made up his class work and graduated near the top of his class. And he immersed himself in his art career with newfound maturity and humility. By some stroke of good fortune his paintings were enormously popular, and drew large sales at galleries.

Now, he stood staring at the series of charcoal images on his picture board. He blinked in surprise. The images were good. Really, really good, showing an emotional depth that was so difficult to transfer from mind and heart to hand. After so many years as an artist, he knew when he had captured the true essence of a given subject's being, and when it was only above mediocre.

The first sketch was a collage of images of Lizzie and Sammie playing on the back porch. The sharing and love shined through as the tiny girl handed her silent friend a small toy truck. The dump trucks were filled with dolls as the children pushed them with no formal rights or wrongs. The comradery of children's play as dirt clung to sweating hands and smiling faces. If he had to have a title this collage would read, *Simply Children*.

The second one was a painting of the older cowboy-looking Hank as he bent over the stove making breakfast. The large calloused hands held an iron skillet filled with pancakes made into Mickey Mouse features. The tough tenderness of boots and chambray contrasted vividly with the everyday chore of fixing food in a family kitchen.

And his favorite was one in which he had mingled his own

experiences with Leeann's. It showed the back of Leeann facing the orange-gold of the rising sun in morning prayer. Just the edges of light touched the mixed color of platinum, blonde and auburn showing in her long striking hair as she watched the yellow dawn paint the dark sky.

He took a deep breath and expelled it slowly. He felt his heart racing as he viewed the special drawings. There was satisfaction in knowing that he had captured on canvas a fleeting never-to-be-repeated moment in time.

These would never be for sale. These were love stories.

CHAPTER NINE

Some sound woke him, a shuffling and a tiny sob. Leeann was up? Or Lizzie? He rolled over to look at the clock. Two-thirty in the morning. Whoever it was sounded distressed, but trying to hold it together without waking anyone. He quickly pulled on his jeans and a warm shirt to quietly slip out of the room. His bare feet made no sound as he moved down the stairway.

Leeann was standing by a chair nearest her bedroom, garbed in a robe and crying softy into a tissue. Multiple tissues lay used in the small basket beside the chair giving evidence that she had been there for some time.

Bob deliberately made a noise as he came down the last stair. "Can't sleep?" he asked softly. "Would tea or chocolate help?"

"Yes, no, I don't know" Leanne sniffed, wiping her face with both hands.

Bob touched the back of her shoulder telling himself that he was simply offering small comfort. She turned into him, laying her head on his chest, making his heart beat double time. He held her lightly, wanting to give solace and not add to her distress.

"I'm so ... so muddled," Leeann choked out. "I hated Leroy. He was a monster to me and the children for the last couple of years. To everyone really. And I feel guilty about him being dead because I've often wished for that very thing. He's Lizzie's father, and I should at least mourn his passing a little. But I can't. Mourning would mean I care, and I don't." She sniffled, the tears slowing. "I don't even know why I'm so sad."

"Emotions don't have to make sense," Bob offered, keeping his voice soft. "Sometimes they aren't logical at all. And the emotion of grief doesn't have to make sense. Grieving over what might have been hurts most I think. All the lost possibilities, and the lost *wants* that never was. And now can never be."

He paused for a moment, lost in his own emotions and the lingering effects of his earlier thoughts. "Emotions are so odd. When my wife finally died all I felt was numb. I kept my feelings to myself, not allowing myself any feelings. If I felt, I would have to deal with those emotions. It was easier to tuck them completely away."

As he said the truth aloud, Bob suddenly realized that maybe the answer to his inability to resume his painting career was simple. Painting was a pouring of emotional self onto a canvas. With the numbness he had felt, there had been nothing of value to offer. No sensations, or passions. Nothing to share with anyone that he wanted them to see. All he had was the ugly side of himself, and who wanted to paint a painful exposure?

He put those thoughts away temporarily as he continued to hold Leeann. As her physical warmth begin to effect his lower body, he slowly stepped back. He allowed himself to press a quick touch of his lips to her forehead. What he wanted was to fit her entire body the length of his, but he knew instinctively that Leeann would panic, and he wasn't ready either. She had been through a sham marriage, bore a child, yet was an innocent in regard to male attention. Slowly, he reminded himself, slowly.

"Let's sit and talk for awhile," Bob suggested. "Maybe talking through our problems will help you sleep." He guided her to the nearest sofa, being careful to keep his arm around her for support. He sat in the chair parallel to her, near but not in touching distance.

"I'm too tired to sleep," Leeann admitted. "I've tried to sort out my feelings into little piles but they don't stay in their proper piles very long. They keep shifting around."

She closed her eyes momentarily. "I hated Leroy, but then I remember that he wasn't all bad. Before Granny Violet died, he never hit. Oh, he wasn't like really good to us or anything, but he wasn't so mean either. He didn't yell at the kids much, and he tried to keep enough food in the house for us. It was only after she died that he and his brothers got worse and worse, until they weren't human anymore."

"In a crazy kind of way I get that, Leeann. I told you that I was married before. We married for the wrong reasons. We were too young to know what compromise was, and had nothing in common. I wanted to build my career which takes solitude, and she wanted to socialize and hang with friends. I was too busy with my own career, and she needed lots of individual attention."

"Would you tell me about it?" Leeann asked softly. "I like you so much and I want to understand your life better."

Bob was taken back by the innocence of her statement. And in all things he must remain honest. To himself and to Leeann.

"I'm a selfish bastard, and I was too intense for her to have the kind of life she wanted. We were the age old dichotomy of chalk and cheese." At Leeann's blank look, he explained, "We were opposites, nothing alike and with clashing differences." Bob looked away, needing to tell Leeann, but knowing that he was certainly not blameless.

"She came and told me she was pregnant. Whether it was mine or not doesn't matter, I wanted that baby with everything in me. She wanted to get an abortion, and we had a big fight about it. She stormed out of the house, got in her sports car, and went racing down the driveway. She crashed into a tree a couple of miles away. I heard the crash."

He closed his eyes, letting the residual pain wash over him. "She was badly injured, lost the baby, and no matter how many doctors or surgeries she had, she was a total invalid. I hired nurses, but in the end I took care of her with the help of our long time housekeeper. She died three years ago of a blood clot."

He opened his eyes to stare directly at Leeann. "I've relived that fight hundreds of times in my mind. I was caught in a trap of my own making and self-interest. And I deserved whatever penance I had to do."

Leeann was quiet for several minutes. "Your fault? When she was angry she drove off in a car, crashed it, and that was your fault?"

With a deep sigh, Bob admitted, "I didn't tell you the worst part. She was never aware of it, even after she was injured, but I was in the process of seeking a divorce before I knew she was pregnant."

"It's hard for me to understand her," Leeann admitted. "I have no experience being what you call happy or not. I'm not sure how happy feels. My happiness was making sure that Lizzie and Sammie were safe and fed. My life has been about survival, getting through the day and then the night, but it seems to me that driving when you're angry is not very smart."

"True," Bob said quietly. "Its not. I wanted you to know me, though. I'm told that I'm somewhat like my cousin Kamon when its necessary. Now I'm going to change the subject. Are you ready for some hot chocolate or maybe some chamomile tea? It'll help you sleep."

"I'm ready to sleep now," Leeann gave a wan smile. "Thank you for tell me about your past. I know it was to keep my mind from going to a dark place, and I do thank you." She touched his arm, went into her bedroom and shut the door.

Bob laid a hand on his arm in the same place her fingers had been. What in the hell had he just done, blurting out his marital past to Leeann? His problems had been minor compared to the life she had lived. He had always had his families love, and the physical well being that money could buy. Food and safety had never even been on his radar.

What an idiot he was. He had never discussed the details of his marriage with anyone. Catherine Ramsey with her gift of Second Sight knew some of it as had Tillie, his long-time house-keeper. When he had decided to relocate, Tillie had chosen to take the retirement package he had offered her, and moved into a mobile home park for seniors. He made a mental note to himself to call her and see how she was doing.

Bob moved to the comfortable leather recliner, put his feet, up and tried to relax. Before he had unloaded his past on Leeann, he had made a discovery. Now he considered the possibility if it was the truth or not.

Maybe the reason he had lost the driving desire to paint had been because his feelings had become deadened. Blunted. He had listened to Jennifer spew allegations of his shortcomings in her pain and frustration, wanting her life back the way it had been before the accident. Had he internalized her bitter rantings and believed her diatribes? Was he that stupid and brainless?

Or had the years of guilt, misplaced or not, worn him down as he had cared for her until he could not defend himself, even to himself? Was that the only way he could protect himself from the relentless day to day caring for her?

Telling Leeann, wanting her to know the real, but flawed Bob Neal, had put a crack in his state of mind. And maybe some peace for his restless soul.

Sometime during the night he pulled a blanket throw over himself and slept on.

"Mr. Bob, Mr. Bob," insisted the child voice. "Momma says if you want to eat you gots to get up now. Momma said."

Bob stretch and yawned. Leeann said he had to get up? "What?'

"Lizzy, what in the world are you doing? Leave Mr. Bob alone. I told you not to come in here," Leeann scolded from the doorway.

Bob gave a slow grin. Damn he felt good. A new day. Maybe talking about the past had actually helped him to move on, like a mini therapy session.

"I wasn't sleeping," he lied. "Lizzy and Sammie came to tell me that it was time to eat."

Leeann narrowed her eyes first at him then at Lizzy. "Humph," she sniffed in disbelieve, returning to the kitchen.

Bob joined the children, Leeann, Hank and Louise at the kitchen table. The mixed matched group made up an oddball kind of family unit, but it felt right somehow. Comfortable even.

The rest of the week was quiet with him and Hank doing morning chores. The children split their time between following one of them around, and sitting on the floor of the garage to watch the 'drop off dog' and her newborn puppies.

Every evening after the children were in bed, Leeann continued to join Bob to watch a documentary or a television program. He tried to keep the evenings as casual and informative as possible without displaying his own ever-growing feelings for her.

He explained the documentary menu and suggested she choose what she wanted. She chose a diverse set of programs to view. Her first was on the anatomy of a Down Syndrome child like Sammie, then how use use Microsoft word on the computer, and on to something
different.

Then she discovered Ted Talks which gave her a wider variety of up to date subjects. She loved the nutrition talk, hated the one on how to become a politician, cried all the way though hunting lions in Africa, and totally dismissed the talk on country life as "the lady doesn't have a clue". Every night's program was new and exciting for her. She seemed to thirst for knowledge of any kind, mulling over each subject as if it was a national security issue.

Bob loved it all. Leeann's mind was a constant wonder to him. His admiration for her increased daily as did his affection. Her innocent touches made his heart beat faster and the future look brighter. He wanted to hug her tightly, keep her in a box for her own safety, and beg her to stay. Unfortunately, none of that was possible.

"We keeping the momma dog and all those puppies?" asked Hank one morning. "If we are, we need to take her and the pups to the Vet to have them checked out and given shots. And to see if they were dropped off, or she got lost. She might have an owner chip. That little mama dog might belong to someone else that misses her."

"I never even thought of that. If she's just lost, we have to do the right thing and give her back, which quite frankly, I would hate to do," Bob admitted. "Let's go as soon as possible."

Lizzy begged to go along with them, but if the momma dog had an owner, Lizzie might be devastated having to give all of the dog family to another home. She and Sammie spent a couple of hours a day sitting in the nearby chairs, watching the puppies starting to play with each other. Sammie sometimes fell asleep watching.

"Would you ladies keep Hugo in the house until we get back?" asked Bob. "He's trying to crawl in the truck with the momma dog."

"Sure," Louise said as she grabbed Hugo's collar, but the large male dog was having none of it. As soon as she had ahold of his collar, he simply pulled her with him toward the truck. It took Hank, Bob, and Louise to finally push Hugo inside where Louise offered him a doggie treat. Leeann's eyes were dancing in merriment along with the giggles of Lizzie as the three adults tussled with the large dog.

Bob and Hank returned a couple of hours later with a tired momma dog, her three puppies, and a truck bed full of doggie merchandise.

"The momma dog belonged to Mrs. Benson who died several months ago," Hank related to the group. "The Vet Tech said that he had seen the little dog around town, but no one seemed to own her now. Her records show that her name is Trixie. We put up a sign with a phone number just in case someone claims her, but Dr. Caldwell said that more than likely she had been living on the street. He gave her a bunch of shots."

"And this," he waved his hand before the pile of dog beds, bags of food, sacks of doggie toys, and several metal containers, "is what happened when Bob decided to go into Joe's Feed and Seed alone. Joe saw him coming," he laughed.

Bob grinned, loving the comradery of being teased by his hired friend. He didn't care. He now had people in his life that he enjoyed being around. He spoke directly to Lizzie and Sammie,

"We're going to keep her, so now we have to call her by her name, Trixie."

"Trixie. I like that name. Don't you, Sammie?" Sammie nodded slightly so Lizzie continued, "Trixie is what I would have thought of if I coulda' named her."

"That is a good name," smiled Louise, going along with the outspoken Lizzie.

Everyone nodded their heads in agreement. It would take awhile before Trixie was accustomed to her new owners, but in the meantime she would be well loved and well fed.

"What about the puppies. Can we name them?" Lizzie asked Hank.

"I think they have to be a little older before they get a name," Hank said, knowing that they probably would be adopted by someone else who would give them names.

The ringing of Bob's phone had everyone else carrying Trixie's doggie beds, and the rest of the merchandize to the garage.

"That was Deke," he explained. "Catherine and Raina want to know if tomorrow would be a good time for them to come down and meet you, Leeann. Saturday is a good time for them, there's less people."

Not willing to explain the remark, he continued, "Both their husbands will come also. Catherine has asked if it was possible for Louise and Hank to take Lizzie and Sammie to McDonald's for lunch? Maybe afterward to Walmart shopping, or to the park? Would that be all right with all of you?"

"You know we would take good care of them, Leeann. It would give you people a chance to talk, and be a new experience for Lizzie and Sammie," inserted Hank.

"Sure, that would be fine. They both know you and Louise. I want them to learn about other people and places. You will make Lizzie mind, won't you?" she insisted. "She's bossy."

The adults all grinned back at her. There was nothing to reply to the true statement.

The next morning Lizzie and Sammie were so excited to

go with Hank and Louise that helping them dress was a problem. They hurried through breakfast, then sat by the door waiting for Hank and Louise to hurry up.

Lizzy had no idea exactly what McDonalds was, but they had seen a commercial on television about Big Macs, and food was a priority for both of the children. It would probably take some time until they understood that food would always be available to them now they no longer lived in the tiny back country settlement.

CHAPTER TEN

Leeann was a nervous wreck as the children left. She had never spent a single day without Lizzie since she was born, and Sammie had been with her constantly since Granny Violet died. There was no one to leave them with, and no one she would have trusted anyway. If she went anywhere, even to the back garden in the woods, Lizzie and Sammie went with her.

And Brenna's sisters wanted to meet her. Bob had told her that the youngest sister, Raina, was something of a historian, although she knew the meaning of the word, she was unsure how it related to her. Now she stood on the porch beside Bob, watching several vehicles approach.

Deke's pickup pulled up in the front of the house, two large cars following it closely. A handsome dark-haired man emerged from the driver's seat of the first one, and moved around to open the passenger car door. A petite, pretty woman with a mass of curly black ringlets got out of the car to take the hand of the large, smiling man.

A tall slim Native American man with long braided black hair and golden-brown skin emerged from the second car. He opened the passenger door for a gorgeous woman with a cap of white-blond hair and an angelic face. The woman lightly touched the man's face before walking forward.

Brenna emerged from the pickup, to join the two other women. Deke waited beside the truck for the two men, then they all followed the women toward the house.

Good grief, what pretty people, was Leeann's first thought. They're prettier than that magazine mama used to have. And all so different looking.

"Good morning," Brenna called, happiness in her voice as she walked besides her sisters.

"Good morning," Leeann said simultaneously with Bob.

"Leeann, this is my sister, Catherine and her husband Trent", she said drawing the petite woman forward with the large good looking man. "And this is my sister, Raina, and her husband Kamon," she indicated the beautiful blond woman and the attractive Native looking man. Only up close could Leeann see the two thin scars slashing from his left eyebrow to his cheekbones. Surprisingly, the scar added to the striking face rather than detracting from it.

"Come in, come in." Bob urged holding the door. He indicated for Leeann to lead the way. Leeann heard a slight gasp behind her from Raina, as Raina reached out and touched her.

"Sorry, I wasn't watching where I was going, and my clumsy self tripped over my own feet," Raina apologized.

Several of the group glanced her way but said nothing. Kamon simply put his hand on his wife's arm and walked closely by her side.

"Brenna, do you want to meet in the kitchen?" asked Leeann. "Louise made banana-nut bread and cinnamon rolls along with coffee in case anyone needs it."

"Are you serious? Louise's cinnamon rolls are awesome, it's want not need," Brenna laughed as she led the way into the kitchen.

Leeann placed the still warm breakfast treats on the table and got out the cups, plates and napkins while everyone seated themselves. Bob and Deke took the end seats with Kamon between Raina and Catherine. They were seated across from Trent and Brenna. The only seat left on the wide bench was directly across from Raina.

Raina immediately took charge of the conversation after explaining that they couldn't stay very long.

"Leeann, I know that Bob told you that I am interested in the history of the area. He also told me that you, your mother,

95

and grandmother had all been born in the hills near the little community of North Fork way back in the hills. And that your great-grandmother had also lived there. And you all had lived together. Can you tell me about them? Their names and that kind of thing?"

"Of course. I was really young, maybe four or five, when my great-grandmother passed so I don't remember her very well, but she was old. After my dad died when I was eight, we lived with my Grandmother Johnson, her sister-in-law Violet Johnson who we call Granny Violet, my mother and me."

Leeann paused to take a deep breath. "My Grandmother Johnson's name was Lily Ann, she died when I was about twelve. My mother died when I was fourteen. My mother's name was Claire Ann Johnson Singer. My dad was John Calvin Singer. Granny Violet died a couple of years ago. I don't know her maiden name, but she was somehow related to the Downey's."

"Do you have any idea where your great-grandmother was from?" asked Raina. "What her maiden name was?"

"No, I don't know where she lived before, but her name was Anna. Anna Rush, but that was her married name."

Raina gave a little gasp. Kamon placed a hand on Raina's arm, gently rubbing it. She didn't look his way but covered his hand with one of her own.

"It sometimes helps to close your eyes with this next question," Raina continued softly. "Tell me everything you remember about your great-grandmother; how she talked, and smelled, and looked."

Leeann obediently closed her eyes, letting her mind drift back to her earliest memories. "She had grey hair but it was streaked looking, kind of like mine but faded, and she had blue eyes I think, but I'm not sure. She was taller than my own grandmother even when she was old. She talked really soft, and I remember my momma saying that her health had never been good. Oh, and her speech was odd sometimes. Especially if she was excited."

"In what way was her speech odd?" asked Raina gently.

"I can't explain it well because I don't know. I never heard anyone else sound like that. It was just different, hard for me to understand her sometimes," Leeann said, her eyes still closed.

"Ye not ken?" asked Raina with a Scottish burr.

Leeann's eyes flew open. "Yes," she almost shouted. "She sounded exactly like that." Turning to Bob, she asked, "What does it mean?" Tears gathered in her eyes.

"Bob, before you answer," Raina went on interrupting Bob before he could speak, "I need to ask Leeann something else," She was silent for a moment then asked, "Did anyone ever ask you to memorize a saying, or an old story? Or maybe a myth?"

"I'm not suppose to discuss stuff like that." Leeann immediately became defensive and sat up straighter. "My mother made me swear. A blood oath with a death penalty," she admitted turning her palm over to reveal a faint scar in the the fleshy part of her thumb.

Tears were silently rolling down Catherine's cheeks, while Brenna swallowed a couple of times, wiping her eyes on her sleeve. Deke silently handed her a napkin from the table.

"Kamon?" asked Raina, her eyes glimmering with unshed tears.

Leeann looked at the man sitting completely still beside Raina. His voice was deep and serious as he answered, looking directly into Leeann's eyes. "Yes. She is. It's all true, everything she said."

Leeann looked from one person to another, but all other eyes were on the pretty dark-haired woman Catherine.

"You have taken the blood oath of all of the people who have gone before and of all the people who will come after. Your heritage was taken from you through no fault of your own," Catherine said solemnly, tears on her face.

Leeann felt a shiver run down her spine. She had no understanding of what was happening, or what Catherine was inferring, but what ever it was she would try to comply. Catherine was one powerful lady. She had never experienced the kind of awe she felt, not fearfulness like from the Downey's, but rather a wonderment toward a deeply compelling spiritual person.

"I have no idea of how much history you have had or what you understand of the past," Catherine said quietly. "Do you know about Second Sight?"

Leeann nodded. "My mother explained that it was the ability to see some things in the future." An intake of breath was barely audible from the group. A mother passing on information of a unique gift was highly unusual to say the least.

"Your mother was wise," Catherine continued ignoring the others. "That's a good definition. Because of a girl-woman who lived a long time ago, a group of Scottish clan members migrated to the Americas and settled in the mountains near here. They intermarried with the local Native Americans who had a clan system similar to their own, creating a unique blend of cultures and a tribal clan." Catherine glanced at Brenna.

"And I can't See you," added Catherine. "I have the gift of Second Sight, among other things, and I can focus on a peripheral person and gain some insight to those near unless they are related to me, like Bob. I've tried to use both Hank and Louise and I simply can't Know you at all through my sight."

Brenna took up the story, "And I have not been entirely truthful with you. I am a Healer with gifts beyond my training as a physician. Normally, or abnormally as the case may be, I can examine a person and can feel if anything is out of the ordinary internally, a wrongness for want of a better word. It's very strong and always true. With you, it isn't. It's faint, like a distant drum beat."

"What does all of that mean?" Leeann asked worriedly. "Are you saying I'm somehow not right, or something is wrong with me?" she asked, jumping to conclusions.

"Raina?" Catherine asked. Turning to Leeann, she added in a lighter tone, "Raina is interested in our tribal clan's history, but she is also a truth teller, a person who can feel when a person is not telling the truth. And she never lies. She simply can't. So whatever she says, you can be assured that it is the truth."

"And I say that you are completely fine," Raina assured her."

There's nothing wrong with you. Absolutely nothing." She took a deep breath, letting it out slowly. "As we have said, I've always been interested in the history of our tribal clan. There are ancestor's journals that I've read and reread over the years. A particular story in one of the journals has always haunted me."

She hesitated for another moment, "Our grandmother's young aunt disappeared from Shadow Valley, her home high in the mountains, when she was a young teenager. The clan searched everywhere, even brought in dogs from Scotland. There was never a clue, and it was finally concluded that she had probably had an accident and died somewhere in the valley. But in truth, we don't know if she died, ran away, or was abducted. Her name was Anna Claire Ramsey. Your great-grandmother."

Raina let the silence reign for several long minutes as each person thought through all this meant. Not only to themselves, but for Leeann and her children.

"I ... I don't even know what to say? She ran away? Why would she do that? My great-grandmother was related to all of you? Does that mean that I'm some sort of distant cousin?" she asked in disbelief.

"Actually," Catherine said deliberately, "because this tribal clan, *your* tribal clan," she emphasized, "it doesn't work quite like that. We are more like first cousins or brothers and sisters, the Native American kinship system. Your legal name is Leeann Ramsey, and Lizzy is also a Ramsey. All Ramsey females keep the Ramsey last name. Their son's names are the last name of their husbands."

"And it took some of us a while to get used to that," commented Trent wryly.

"Oh my," breathed Leeann, putting her hands to her face. "I can't believe it. My last name is Ramsey." Tears ran down her cheeks as she smiled. "Lizzie isn't an out-of-wedlock child, she's a Ramsey."

"Bob, I have family," she laughed from her tears. Her eyes widened as another factor hit her. "Am I related to all of you men?"

"You are distantly related to Bob and Kamon. They are from associate clans which probably makes no sense to you right now, but you'll learn."

"Kamon?" asked Catherine, making the choice his.

"We are going to overwhelm you," said Kamon softly, looking directly into her Leeann's eyes. "Simply put, I am Catherine's Ramsey's chosen War Commander. I also have the gift as a Native American Mind Walker, a throw-back skill from some long ago ancestor. I have to have permission from either Catherine or the Council to use that gift."

"And Deke and I were smart enough to marry these ladies," Trent said in a stage whisper, "so we're related by marriage. Catherine and I have two children now, Alexa and Gabe, and Deke and Brenna have two, Brandon and Kassia, that I hear you've already met. Raina and Kamon have four children," he grinned.

Leeann couldn't stop herself from looking at the youthful Raina. "Four?" she whispered.

Raina grinned broadly, laying her head on Kamon's shoulder. "We've been married for almost three years, have twin boys a little over two, and twin baby girls."

Kamon had turned to look at Raina while she explained their family. "And I'm the luckiest man living," he said directly to Raina, seemingly oblivious of the rest of the group as he put his arm around her to pull her closer to his side.

"And they are always like this, so I won't apologize for them," teased Brenna, rolling her eyes.

Raina continued, her hand firmly in Kamon's. "The rest of your story is that you belong to a tribal clan that is philanthropic. For the last two hundred fifty years, we have been Helpers, mostly by using money, but sometimes using power, or strength, or a network of friends. And Leeann, you don't seem to be shocked by the unusual gifts of Brenna and Catherine."

"Actually I'm not. My grandmother told us about people like that in the Bible that have special gifts. She even showed us. Granny Violet didn't believe it, but momma and I did. We figured that if it was in the Bible, maybe a few people could still do some of those things. Momma told me to never discuss anything with anyone, not Granny Violet or anyone else."

"I can't ask how much you know because I don't know how to direct the questions," mused Raina. "I suspect that your great-grandmother did not leave Shadow Valley of her own will, but was kidnapped by someone. Back then there were no phones, or easy communications. There was no way to look for a lost person except to do individual hunts." She sighed, "A Seer cannot view the people they are related to, or that they love. And at that time our own Grandmother was young and lived in Scotland, so there were no clan Seer in Shadow Valley anyway."

"Momma said that Grandmother Johnson told her that when she was a little girl she lived much further back in the hills. She said that her mother, great-grandmother Rush, had home-schooled her, and she saw very few people. My grandmother said she met Gary Johnson because he was a rural mail carrier. They married when she became pregnant with my mother. That's when they moved to Cottonwood Creek, then to the North Fork area."

"That makes sense," inserted Catherine. "Some parts of the mountain were so isolated that you could live years seeing only a few people, especially in her generation. Even in the low altitudes of the mountains in Arkansas, electricity didn't come to all of the areas until the 1940's and 1950's."

"May I ask questions?" Leeann directed the query to Catherine.

Catherine nodded, so Leeann continued, "Would you please tell me where you live, and about your life? You know, what you do every day. All of you. I'm trying to understand but I don't have enough information."

Everyone laughed, Trent's especially loud. "You just said my favorite saying. I never have enough information. Never. And these yahoos have no idea that unless you have it, you really can't make a good decision. Right?" He asked Leeann, with a wide grin.

Leeann smiled happily. She was being treated as if she was

part of this awesome group of people. She had been scared for most of her life. After marrying Leroy, she had been afraid. But after Granny Violet died, she been terrified. She and the children could have dropped off the face of the earth, and no one would have questioned whatever the Downey brothers said happened.

"To answer your question, it's best that you understand the beginning," said Catherine slowly. "As we said before, in the middle of the 1700's a girl-woman ancestor with Second Sight saved the lives of Clan Lords and their followers from mass poisoning. The Clans future existence and historical deeds had already been written in the Book of Time. She was rewarded by our ancient ancestors with the protection for her future generations and any Gifts the Creator bestowed on them."

"With her gift as a Seer, the girl-woman had seen the coming massacre at Culloden where the English brought Scotland to her knees, and forever changed all of Scotland's way of life. She had also Seen the turmoil and potential death of many Scots through starvation and deprivation."

"She advised her children and those others who chose to join them, to move to the new country of the Americas. She said that there they could carve out a hidden valley where they would be able to live with both freedom and peace. And to be able to keep their unique gifts without reprisal from man, and man's made-up laws."

The room was silent as she continued, "The group sailed for the small port of New Orleans, Louisiana, then traveled up the mighty Mississippi River to the White River, then on to its tributaries located in what would years later became the state of Arkansas. The group trudged up a mountain range to one of the most rugged parts of the Ozark Mountains to a small valley, where they settled a community in the forested rocky terrain."

"Only a handful of trappers had ever ventured into the Ozarks at that early time. Native Americans had lived in the local cliffs and forests for hundreds of years however. The Osage, and later the Cherokee and Choctaw, mixed freely with the new arrivals. The Scottish people have always married into the local populations wherever they traveled. As they intermingled tribes and clans, both groups were forever changed into one. Okay so far? You looked confused and mystified there for several minutes."

CHAPTER ELEVEN

"Then it isn't a made-up story?" Leeann asked, new tears streaming down her cheeks. "My mother made me memorize that story as my grandmother had made her. And that I swore on my mother's honor that if I ever had a child that I would pass the story on."

"She told you about the girl-woman, and the migration?" At Leeann's solemn nod, Catherine asked, "What else did she make you memorize?

"How did you know? That there was more?" asked Leeann hesitantly. "That's why there was a blood bond. So that I would remember that I was not supposed to tell anyone, no matter who or what they were."

Brenna smiled softly. "You can tell us, Leeann. We are all cousins. You are our cousin and in our tribal clan that's more like a sister."

Leeann sought to hold back more tears so she could explain. "I'm not sure how much is true, or has been changed in the telling."

Leeann closed her eyes to recapture the long ago memories. "Some of the things were fanciful like a huge manor house make of stone with many rooms and beautiful furniture. Of a valley where there was more than enough to eat for everyone and people shared. That Native Americans and the Scottish people were one people. That there were no murders, or poverty, or thieves there." Leeann opened her eyes to see everyone with wide smiles, even Bob.

Realizing what Leeann must be thinking, he quickly related, "Leeann, we're not laughing at you. We're smiling because that is exactly the way it is in Shadow Valley."

"True," agreed Catherine, "when you go up to the valley you can read the journals of all of your ancestors. Their journals speak of hardships, but also a sense of freedom, of becoming and evolving into who we are. Striving to keep the best of what each clan system was, and intermingling it with our cultures as we mixed our blood."

"This is simply overwhelming," Leeann admitted. She felt Bob's eyes on her. That beautiful man was there for her, willing to help. Her eyes opened wider as she looked up at him. "We're cousins?" Her tone was one of dismay.

Brenna and Raina broke out in giggles while Catherine frowned at both of them. "If you are asking if Bob is a lot related to you, then the answer is no, only distantly. Not enough to count for anything."

"Oh Dang," Raina snapped sharply, reaching for her coat. She turned toward Kamon, who quickly stepped in front of her, blocking her from view as she put on her coat.

"Baby feeding time and you forgot your breast pump?" asked Kamon. "Sorry sweetheart, I should have checked for you." He gave her a quick hug promising, "I'll have you home as soon as possible. I know it's uncomfortable but at least the girls have their bottles." Both of them flung goodbyes to the group as they hurried out.

"Remember when I did that, Trent? I would get involved in my work, and Alexa would not wait. I'd hear her whimper and boom, I'd be a dripping milk-mama," she laughed. "Our son was much better behaved."

"Alexa still can't wait," admitted Trent. "She wants everything yesterday."

"Wonder where she got that?" asked Catherine, glaring at Brenna who held up her hands in protest. "She's exactly like her aunt."

"Stop picking on my wife," kidded Deke. "Her temper has cooled some as has her impatience. Well, it's going to someday," he grinned, when Brenna stuck her tongue out at him.

Leeann knew her face was scarlet. These women laughed with their husbands about breast feeding and babies, even the silent Kamon. That man was fascinating to watch. He seemed to be aware of Raina's every movement. And he touched her. On her arm, or her hand, or her shoulder. Leeann had never seen anything like that. An intense forceful man who almost seemed to be a part of Raina.

She studied the other couples who were a little older. The most reserved one was Catherine sitting across from Trent. A stranger entering the room would know who the leader was, even with the big dynamic men there. Neither man seemed to be mind though. Trent was more extroverted than Deke, but both seemed to dote on their wives.

Beautiful auburn-haired Brenna was self-confident and more outgoing, teasing and poking fun at everyone, especially her cowboy-looking husband. Deke was not as pretty as Catherine's husband Trent, but he was completely masculine with a rangy build and a laid back persona.

Bob was the quietest of the group, the most self-contained. He had the same intensity and sleek body movements as Kamon, both seeming to focus completely on a subject. Also he was the most handsome and sexy. She blushed at her own wayward thoughts.

Catherine rose from the table, and stood with her hand on Trent's shoulder. "I think we've given Leeann much to think through. And I know it has to be overwhelming," Catherine said softly. "I'll call you and we can make plans for you to visit the valley."

"I would love to do that," Leeann said honestly. "In my mind the valley, and all the things in it, was fiction to me. Now that it is a reality, I'm unsure of how to separate the two."

"Then I'll see you both soon," Catherine replied giving first Leeann, then Bob and finally Brenna and Deke a hug. She quickly left, Trent with his arm around her shoulders.

Brenna gave a long sigh. "Catherine can't stay long where a

lot of strangers live," she explained. "She has Second Sight and since she has been in training since childhood, her Knowing is concentrated."

Noting the perplexed look on Leeann's face, she explained, "Catherine says that when she is in an area with a great deal of people it's like turning on a thousand television sets up loud, and setting them at different channels. She is bombarded with the sounds and gets physically sick. Really, really ill."

"She has to stay in a somewhat isolated place?"

"Unfortunately yes. She's known all this since childhood and tested it several times to her body's misfortune. It is easier as our tribal clan's headquarters, for want of a better word, is in Shadow Valley, and that works for her. Trent still flies to New York City occasionally to consult with his business company. He used to own it, but now has reverted to a more minor role, as has Deke."

"Then Deke and Trent knew each other before they married sisters?" Leeann asked. "I'm sorry to ask so many questions, Brenna, but I'm trying to put you all together in my mind to make sense of all today's information."

"Ask away," Brenna replied grinning. "A friend has taken Brandon for the day for a play-date and the baby is napping with Patty. I'm free."

"And I think I'll answer that question," Deke said sharing a glance with Brenna. "Trent and I have been friends since early elementary school. There's also one more of us, Bob Bailey, who is the major owner of our business now. We all met on a rag tag soccer field, bonded, and grew up as brothers. We still have the same bond."

"You grew up in Las Vegas, right?" queried Bob, knowing the answer but wanting Leeann to hear it.

"Oh yeah. Leeann, there is a rule in Shadow Valley that you can only talk about yourself, so I'll tell you about me, which is also similar to Trent's. My parents were alcoholics who worked sporadically, I spent many a night on Trent's couch. We got football scholarships to college. Afterward I worked in a series of initialed law enforcement agencies until my fiancée was accidently killed. I spent a few years in South America and Africa before I met Brenna. Now, I go where she goes."

He gave her a warm secret glance. "I am her bodyguard, husband, and she is everything to me. And as Kamon said, I'm the luckiest person on this earth."

"Actually, I am," countered Brenna. "And Deke can cook," she grinned.

"You can't cook?" Leeann asked, looking in disbelief at Brenna.

"Very, very little," admitted Brenna. "Deke cooks well though."

Leeann shook her head. She couldn't imagine not being able to cook. Her mother had started teaching her when she was so small she stood on a stool to reach the table.

"Does Catherine or Raina cook?" Leeann asked cautiously.

"Catherine, no. And definitely not Trent. Raina is actually a very good cook," Deke answered, "as is Kamon."

Ignoring both men, Leeann looked directly at Brenna. "Kamon seems to be ready to spring into action when he's sitting down. I don't know how to explain it very well."

"Actually you've explained it extremely well. Kamon has had all kind of special training and is a law unto himself. He told you that he is a Native American Mind Walker, which means that he can read other people's thoughts. He was trained by our Grandfather Youngblood in the ethical and honorable use of that gift. He is also Catherine's ceann-cath, which is the number two of the tribal clan. As he told you, he is the war leader, chosen by Catherine."

"I've never heard of the term ceann-cath, but he certainly seems like he could be a warrior."

Bob had remained mostly quiet and now spoke. "Kamon looks like a full blood Native American, but in actuality is at least half Scottish. The warrior instinct that flows through Kamon is of the Highland Scot variety as well as the Native American."

"The Scot's can be more ruthless and relentless than anyone. They always have been. It was about survival," agreed Brenna.

"The blood oath," murmured Bob, glancing at Leeann.

"The blood oath," Leeann repeated.

"Leeann, if you have any questions that Bob can't answer, call me. I'll see you in the next couple of days. By that time, you will have thought of fifteen things you absolutely must know although Bob will be able to answer most of them for you."

After Brenna and Deke left, Bob and Leeann sat quietly at the table. Bob waited to see what she needed after an astonishing week. Leeann's days had included feeling depressed that the father of her child was dead, and ended with belonging to a huge, ancient tribal clan of Scot-Native Americans.

"May I ask you a personal question? You don't have to answer if you don't want."

"Leeann, I have no secrets. Ask anything you want. The only thing is that I can't tell you about other people except in a general way. It's part of the ancient law."

Leeann nodded in agreement. Bowing her head, she asked, "Is there a lady, ahh like a girlfriend, in your life.?" Leeann's face was fiery red.

Bob was prepared to answer questions concerning Shadow Valley or maybe more questions about her past; he was surprised to find that her interest was in him. When she said personal, she meant personal. And his heart had taken a major leap with her interest in him.

"No I don't. I haven't for five years. Not since Jennifer's car accident."

"You said I could ask you anything and I want to know about you. Not your past necessarily, but you inside. How you feel and think and stuff," she said.

"Are you asking if I loved her so much that I couldn't be with anyone else?" asked Bob, his eyes sparkling.

"Yes, I think I am. And I do know that I shouldn't ask that," she grinned unrepentant, wanting an answer and ignoring her reddening face.

"Then the answer is no. I'm not sure I was ever in love with her at all. But in lust. Yes, most definitely in lust," he grinned as he watched Leeann's face become even more red.

"I've never been either of those," Leeann admitted. "My mother loved my father, but that's the only positive man-woman relationship that I've seen."

"Was there a reason you asked Leeann?"

"Well, I was curious of course, but I saw those three couples and I've never been around something like that." She gave a heartfelt sigh. "Bob, I want that. I thought there was such a special bond between Deke and Brenna, and Catherine and Trent, but Kamon and Raina's seems stronger somehow."

"I agree whole heartedly with you Leeann. I want that too," he admitted. "Catherine told me I could answer any of your questions. When Ramsey women mate there is a bond between her and her mate, whether the mating has been by force or not. If it is by force and there is no love, there is not a child. If it is a love match, a strong spiritual and physical bond is formed in which they each share the essence of the other person." Bob fell quiet letting Leeann take the next step in working through her own circumstances.

Leeann chewed on her lower lip, letting several minutes pass. "I'm suppose to be a Ramsey, but I had a child by force with Leroy Downey. What does that mean?"

"I don't know and quite frankly I doubt if anyone else does either. I've read many of our ancestor's journals recording their histories but I've never come across anything like yours," he admitted being as honest as possible.

"Do you think it means that I can never have another child if I love someone? Or that none of the Ramsey women's heritage is mine? Or ..."

"Whoa, let's not jump to conclusions. We don't know

what our Destiny is at the moment. It's going to take time."

"I love children. I didn't want any more of Leroy's children, but I would like to have several more."

"And you may," Bob argued. "And Lizzy is awesome. So is Sammie."

Frowning Leeann asked, "How about one more question."

"Anything," Bob answered. He was thrilled that she wanted to know more about him as a man. He was getting the feeling that she was as fascinated by him as he was by her.

"You are part Native American, like Kamon, right?"

"Yes, we probably have about the same degree of Scottish and Native American blood. The really interesting part is that you Ramsey women, and Leeann, you are a Ramsey woman, may have more Native American blood than either of us."

"Bob, I'm a Ramsey," she whispered. "I'm a Ramsey," she repeated, hugging herself
tightly.

"Yes, you are," Bob chuckled. He couldn't contain the happy grin as he looked at Leeann, a smile on her face and dancing eyes.

"I'm a Ramsey, but I have to admit that I don't feel as if I am. And I have some Native America blood too?"

"Yes you do, although I'm unsure of how much, as all of your male ancestors have to be taken into account too. That has to include your great-grandfather, grandfather, and father," he explained.

"Dang, as Hank would say," she laughed.

"I'm from the Cherokee-Osage tribes. The history of the Cherokee's says they came through the northern part of Arkansas during the Trail of Tears. Many, many people have Cherokee blood even if only a smidgen. John Ross, the elected Chief of the Cherokee Nation for years was one eighth Cherokee, according to their history."

Bob frowned in thought. "For me, I think that blood makes

very little difference, it's about where the heart sings inside a person that counts."

Hearing a car drive up, Leeann grinned at Bob, "Ready for the onslaught? Lizzie will have to tell us everything she did, who said what, and how she felt."

Leeann laughed aloud with happiness she couldn't contain. What a day. She had family, cousins, and Bob had said "us" referring to Lizzy.

The next hour was spent listening to every detail of where Lizzy, Sammie, Louise and Hank had gone that day. From there it had been a never-take-a-breath recitation of all that they had done, thought, felt, and ate. Finally, Lizzie wound down ending her monologue with, "Oh Momma. It was the bestest day ever."

After the children were in bed that night, Leeann wandered out into the living room foyer. She felt restless and anxious for no reason. For the first time that she could remember, she didn't expect disaster in her live. And it was disconcerting.

She had lived in very real fear most of her life, fear that had a great chance that it could become true. The fear that her ill father would not survive, then the fear that she was alone in the world after her mother died. Then the overwhelming physical fear of Leroy and his brothers.

Fear was paralyzing. The mind froze, mired in deep ice. The body cringed even when is remained still, trying not to bring attention to itself. The skin tingled just under the surface, waiting for the first blow that was inevitable. No wonder that leaving isn't an option until the survival mode kicks in. Only when the choice was 'stay and most likely die, or run and maybe have a chance to live' could action be taken.

"Is something wrong?" asked the soft voice behind her.

"No, truthfully there isn't and that's what's wrong, which makes no sense at all," she told Bob, turning to look at the too handsome man.

"I guess I've felt on edge for so long that now it's like a fairy tale. Leroy is dead, although I have a hard time believing it all the time. I have a history and the possibility of a new family. I have new friends, and I know that my future is the best it's ever been." She forced her eyes to met his. "So why am I upset and feeling like I've lost something?"

Bob quietly thought through Leeann's world, past and present, taking the question as seriously as it had been asked.

"Do you think that part of the problem may be that you have no way of knowing where your next step will be? That the unknown is out there? Whatever that is."

Leeann gave that some thought. She sat down in a nearby chair and indicated that Bob should take the other. "The unknown is certainly out there. And I don't know anything. Bob, I don't even know what I don't know," she snorted.

Bob grinned at the funny little sound she made. "When you were younger, before Leroy became violent, you knew what was expected of you. You were a kid, so someone made the decisions for you. Now they don't. You have to make decisions based on what you want. And I would guess that everything that you do know, is mostly what you don't want, right?" Bob asked softly emphasizing the don't.

"True, what I want is to ask questions and someone give me a straight answer, even though it may not be the one I want to hear. A completely honest answer to whatever I want to ask."

She held his gaze, making sure that he was truly listening. "Would you do that for me? I know that it's improper."

"Leeann, I will answer whatever you ask, big and small, as honestly and as candid as I can be," Bob interrupted.

"Candid means sincerely, right?"

"Yes, that what it means."

"Do you think that I'm going to lose Sammy?"

"That could probably be best answered by Brenna who also would give you an honest answer. For me, I think we will lose him sometime in childhood, but we will do everything we can to make all the year's good years. As Brenna told us, he has a lot of medical problems that are not treatable, especially heart failure. And he's not a candidate for surgery."

Leeann nibbled on her bottom lip to keep her emotions in. "I knew it, but didn't want to admit it. The older he gets, the more problems he has."

"What we can do, what Brenna will do, is give him the absolute best care in the world. He's such a happy, precious little boy. If there comes a time when something can be done, then we will do it."

"He is so sweet," agreed Leeann blinking rapidly.

"And Leeann, we may get lucky and he will be with us for a long, long time. As the Creator destines."

Leeann nodded in understand, then moved to a different subject. "A long time ago people would ask me *what* I wanted to be when I grew up. I thought that was odd. I wanted to tell them *who* I wanted to be when I grew up. You know, the kind of person I would want to become. I still don't know exactly, even with knowing some of my background, but basically I want to live to become someone that I would be proud to be," she laughed lightly.

"When my life is past, I want it to be said simply 'well done'. Not because I have the most power, or money, or local prestige, but because I gave life as much as I could." She paused. "You know, like what someone smart wrote, 'I left the earth a little better than it would have been if I hadn't been born'."

Bob could only look and admire someone so special that after the crappy hand she had been dealt so far, she had the depth of emotion she did.

The evening passed with Leeann asking questions and Bob trying to answer them as truthfully as possible. They shared stories about Lizzie, and Trixie's pups, the new foods that were favorites of the children. Anything that she wanted to talk about, he was willing to listen as it gave him more insight into who she was, and wasn't.

Bob heard the clock chime 12 o'clock and with some reluctance bide Leeann goodnight. His heart felt light as she asked if they could talk each night with her questions. She beamed at his quick positive nod.

The nightly sessions continued with Leeann asking questions. She also wanted to view more documentaries on different subjects. When Bob suggested sticking to the present day documentaries, Leeann was in giggles saying, "Bob, it's all present to me. I never knew any of this existed." So they watched whatever she wanted to watch; which was everything from slapstick comedy to Macy parade reruns to climate change, and she asked questions. Lots and lots of questions. Old or new, past or present, Leeann was enthralled with all her new knowledge.

And Bob was enthralled with Leeann. He actually liked her as a person. She was beautiful but didn't know it, and honest without judgements. And she was smart, absorbing information like a sponge, and wanting to discuss whatever it was aloud.

Most of the time he knew the answers to her 'whys' but occasionally he had to look up the information on his iPhone. Each day was a wonder for Bob as he shared his thoughts, and beliefs with eager-to-know-everything Leeann.

The only problem that he had not foreseen was his body's automatic reaction to Leeann's casual touches. He didn't know if she was conscious of what she was doing, or it was simply unplanned gestures. Her sweet smile and the way she watched him made his body heat and his heart beat faster. She sometimes gave him a hug before retiring to her room or a quick peek on the cheek which sent his hormones into overdrive.

And it was driving him crazy. He struggled to keep his physical attraction to Leeann as tamped down as possible. Sometimes he thought she was treating him like an older relative, and at other times he thought that she was learning the female to male relationship in what she thought was a safe environment. If that was the case, then that's what he would give her.

Safety. To learn in a protected environment. She didn't need his recently awakened passion to interfere with her new reality as a Ramsey. She didn't know it yet, but she had the entire world at her fingertips if she so chose.

But he was going to do everything in his power to include him in her choosing.

CHAPTER TWELVE

His world changed with a phone call.

"Bob, this is Kamon. I've just landed at the Spring Creek Airport. Jake Downey escaped from the hospital where he was being treated. He overpowered his guard and beat him so badly that we don't know if the guard is going to make it or not. Catherine has requested that Leeann and the children come to Shadow Valley for a visit immediately. She's calling Leeann."

"And Jake will come after Leeann first," commented Bob, following Kamon's trend of thought. "At least as soon as he can." He could hear the ringing of Leeann's new cell phone in another part of the house.

"True. The authorities seem to think that he will leave the area in order to not be caught. I don't," he said in his hard, firm voice.

"Neither do I. What do you want me to do right now?" interrupted Bob.

Kamon Youngblood was Catherine's ceaan-cath, the War Leader of the tribal clan, therefore the commander when any conflict occurred. Under Scottish law, a ceann-cath could be chosen by the clan leader when the leader could not physically lead the clan into battle. This occurred when there was succession by blood of a young person, or when a clan chose a female as their leader, as in the case of Catherine Ramsey. The ancient law coincided perfectly with the Native American system of leadership. Bob knew that some Native American tribes still chose women as leaders, very capable and astute leaders.

"Just protect everyone until I'm there with a plan. I know

that Grandfather Youngblood insisted that you have training when you were in college. He said that you took to it like a duck to water."

"That summer was the very best of times. I needed a kick in the ass and to get my head on straight. Painting and intense physical warrior training, the best time of both worlds. And Grandfather Youngblood. We were so lucky to have him."

"Yes we were. I'm getting a car now so it should be fifteen minutes or so. I have the gate code and will shut it behind me. Make sure that Leeann, Louise, and the kids are inside the house. And ask Hank to come to the house with his rifle."

Bob called Hank, explaining that Jake Downey had escaped from the hospital, asked him to come to the house immediately and to bring his gun. He could hear Louise and Leeann in the kitchen with Lizzy and Sammie, so he retrieved his own handgun and rifle from the home library safe. He tucked the handgun in the center of his back and placed the rifle on top of the fireplace mantel, well out of reach of the kids but handy. Hank was through the front door by the time he had finished.

"I'll put a video on for the children and watch them if you need some time," Hank said.

"Thanks. Hey, Lizzy and Sammie. Hank wants to see that new video he got for you the other day. He's putting it on right now."

"C'mon Sammie, we gots to see that again," Lizzy urged as she ran out of the kitchen followed by a slower moving Sammie.

"Oh Bob, I was looking for you. Catherine called a few minutes ago. She told me about Jake and asked me to come visit her for awhile. Is that okay?" she asked hesitantly. "I wanted to talk to you first."

"Kamon just called me. He's on his way to get you and the kids. You need to be safe and there's no safer place on earth than Shadow Valley and its wildlife refugee. Go ahead and pack quickly." He paused for a moment, glancing out of the kitchen window. "That was fast, Kamon's here."

Kamon greeted Hank and hurried into the kitchen.

Hank stood in the doorway, watching the kids, but listening to the conversation.

"Leeann, Louise," Kamon addressed each one, then gave them all the information he had. "Jake Downey has escaped from the hospital. He overpowered the sheriff's deputy who was the guard outside his hospital room, and tried to beat him to death. A nurse came by, screamed, and he ran. The deputy is now in the hospital in the Intensive Care Unit. That was two hours ago, and Jake has not been caught. Law enforcement kept it quiet in order not to panic everyone. It was just made public. Dumb decision on their part," he stated firmly.

"Leeann, he has made it very well known that he blames you for both of his brother's deaths, and all his other problems. He knows he's going to prison for life at the very least. And he is now the most dangerous criminal out there. He has nothing to lose," Bob's voice was slow and hard.

"I agree with Bob. He's going to get the same punishment no matter what he does now. More than likely the death penalty which is legal in Arkansas, or at the very least life without parole," Kamon's voice continued in the same vein as Bob's. Both men's face's were without expression, which made their combined announcement more serious and frightening.

"The kids?" Leeann questioned, taking a deep breath, fighting for calm.

"They're fine. You can hear Lizzy giggling. They're safe," Bob assured her.

"And that's the way they are going to stay," asserted Kamon. "Catherine said she called and invited you for a visit to see her," he told Leeann. He stopped for several moments before continuing, "She said to tell you that she needed to see you and the children and you will be totally safe at the wildlife sanctuary."

Before Leeann could ask questions, Bob inserted, "That's a great idea. You'll learn a lot and the kids will also." He hoped that he was telling her enough so that she would know not to ask questions about Shadow Valley in front of Louise and Hank.

Leeann looked steadily back at Bob unblinking, then asked, "When are we suppose to go?"

"Immediately," Kamon answered. "Like now."

"Then I'd better get us packed," stated Leeann without further comment. "Oh, what about Louise and Hank? And you?" she asked Bob with frown.

Kamon answered for Bob. "Some friends of mine are coming to help out. They will stay here at Bob's, and a couple of others will stay with Deke and Brenna. Stubborn Brenna refuses to leave as she says she might be needed as Dr. Farrison is out of town. Sorry to sort of take over but until Jake is caught, no one is safe."

Hank and Louise had been whispering back and forth as they listened to the talk. Now, Hank lifted his hand for attention. "If it's all right with you Bob, Louise and I would like to take a week off, maybe two or so, if Jake isn't caught immediately. You will have enough fire power here, and I really want Louise gone too."

He took a deep breath, then blurted, "Louise has said yes to my marriage proposal. I think this might be a good time to get married in another state, and have a short honeymoon."

"That's wonderful," Bob grinned widely. "Congratulations to you both. And now is the perfect time to be somewhere else that safer. Take as much time as you need. Do you know where you're going?"

"Louise has never been to Las Vegas so we thought we'd go out there. Maybe rent a car and go over to Disneyland."

"I've never been anywhere," admitted Louise. "Never even dreamed of just picking up and going," her eyes sparkled with excitement.

"Me neither," admitted Leeann. "I'm going to visit with Catherine," she grinned at Louise who returned the happy look.

"Pack quickly, please Leeann. We need to get you and the children out of here," encouraged Kamon.

"First I'm going to help you pack, Leeann, then I'm going to call my sister Sarah and tell her that Hank popped the question last night. And I said yes. Then I'm going to pack," Louise beamed at Hank. "You need to pack too, Hank."

"Packing will take me about five minutes," laughed Hank. "I'll be right back," he asserted with his giddy grin.

The ladies rushed to pack for Leeann and the children, both so excited that they laughingly interrupted each other.

"You're flying Leeann and the kids up to Shadow Valley?" asked Bob. With Kamon's affirmative nod, Bob continued, "I envy you. I would love to see Leeann's and kid's faces with flying, and then Shadow Valley with the Stone House. What a shock that will be. Damn, I wish I could go, but it's more important that Jake is captured."

Kamon looked steadily at Bob at the word capture. "However it works out."

"Destiny," Bob agreed, his tone reflecting Kamon's. "However it works out. Now I need to write a honeymoon check for Hank. One very nice thing out of this."

The two men talked quietly as they waited, figuring out how Jake had escaped the hospital unit and if the guard would live. Both of them were in agreement that Jake had little to lose and would stay in the area to enact revenge on all the people he thought had harmed him, and caused the death of his brothers.

Hank returned in ten minutes or so. "It took a little longer but I had to button down the house. I don't know how long we'll be gone," he pronounced happily. When he glanced at the check Bob gave him, he gasped. "I can't take this. Good grief this would buy a car. A really nice car."

"And I hope it'll buy a really nice honeymoon," laughed Bob.

"You know, I've loved that woman my entire life, from grammar school to the present day. I never hoped that this would happen, but I'm so damn happy I could dance."

"Hank you are a terrific dancer, you always have been," Louise declared as she came out with a large suitcase, a carryon, and her purse. "I didn't know what to take so I took lots," she confessed, putting her hands up to her blushing cheeks.

"Nay, take whatever. This is our once in a lifetime forever trip," Hank grinned. "Thanks Bob, for everything. See you Kamon. Louise and I talked it over and decided that we're going to drive for awhile, then decide if we want to fly or just drive to Nevada. Louise wants to see the country, so I guess we'll see," he stated with a shoulder shrug as they hurried out.

"Yeah, right. As if he has a choice. They're going to drive. Period. Whatever makes Louise happy is what he'll do. I've been there," Kamon grinned, "and still am".

The two cousins stood smiling at each other, when Leeann came in. She stopped in the doorway and looked back and forth between them.

"I didn't realize how much you look alike until now. Your facial structure and the way you move, like sleek cats," she exclaimed. Realizing her revealing statement, she blushed a deep red.

"Mama, you're standing in the doorway, I can't go passed," Lizzy complained, dragging a duffel bag. Sammie was right behind her with another smaller one.

"Sorry, Lizzie. Let me carry this suitcase to the truck. I hope you don't mind, Bob, but we borrowed the bags for the children's clothes that Sarah brought. And I guess I'm ready to go," she said softly looking at Bob, her face still pink.

Kamon glanced at the two of them, quietly took the duffel bags and lead the children out of the room.

Knowing that his time to talk was limited, Bob said hurriedly, "Leeann, you have your phone. Call or text me and come back as soon as you want. I want what you want. Whatever is best for you and the children. Stay as long as you want, but know that you'll always have a place here. With me. Always."

He didn't tell her all that was in his heart or what he wanted desperately to say. Come back. Come back and let's see what's happening between us. He didn't have the right to insist on her doing anything; he wished he did but for now, it was what it was.

"Can I phone every night to tell you about my day? Is that

too much? Can I hug you goodbye?" asked Leeann hesitantly. "You've done so much for ..."

"Please don't. Don't say that. I wanted to do whatever you needed. And I hope you call every night. And during the day too. I'm here for whatever you want, whenever you want," he reminded her.

He put his arms around her, drawing her close to his body. She tipped her chin up to look directly into his eyes, and he was lost. He slowly lowered his mouth to gently press hers. When she stood on tip toes to gain more contact, he ran his tongue over the seam between her lips. She parted them ever so slightly and he took the kiss deeper, letting her feel the desire that ran though his body like wildfire. He kissed her several times, finally slowing, as he knew she had to leave.

Leeann looked dazed and wide eyed, touching her lips with her fingertips. She brought her hand up to run her fingertips gently down the side of his face, as if she could memorize his face through looking them. She smiled softly, her eyes shining, then picked up her purse to follow Kamon and the children outside.

Bob watched them leave from his front porch. And prayed that she would want him enough to return. Maybe they would, and they could start something more together. Kissing her was heady stuff, he could only imagine what the feelings of making love would be like. He gave a shake to dislodge the thoughts in his head to focus on the coming possibilities of Jake Downey. For now, his job was to protect. That he had been well trained to do.

Twenty minutes later two men in their early thirties arrived at the gate. They introduced themselves as Matt Johnson and Scott Adams. They explained that they lived in the general area, and that Matt had known Kamon in the military. Scott had laughed and commented that he had served, but not in the same unit. Each of them had a couple of military style guns and had been chosen by Kamon so Bob knew that they would be outstanding at what they had been asked to do.

They visited, checking out each person's expertise, then

made plans for the best way to ensure no one came on the property without their knowledge. Matt told Bob that his parents were deceased and that he took care of his brother and sister, twin high schoolers, but they had gone on a church sponsored trip for the week so he was free to stay as long as needed. His ranch would be fine under the care of his long time foreman and workers. Scott said his mother was his only relative and she lived in Little Rock now, adding "Thank God," under his breath.

The afternoon was spent walking the grounds and monitoring all the cameras that had previously been installed. Matt had taken the four-wheeler out of the barn and made a surveillance in the nearby woods, then rechecked the entry gate to be sure all was okay. They decided to take three hour shifts during the night, mostly to watch the night vision cameras that Kamon, Deke, and he had installed.

In the morning Bob noted that both Matt and Scott were getting as antsy as he was. Maintaining high alert waiting for something to happen was mind wracking, making the mind and body tense. The morning and afternoon were spent in much the same fashion, examining all the outbuildings once again, and scrutinizing the cameras.

At about four o'clock, they heard the gate open and a truck coming up the drive. Prepared for whatever, they were all mildly disappointed when Deke's big black truck came into focus.

"We can all stand down," Deke told the group with a wide grin. "Jake Downey is dead."

"What happened?" interrupted Matt. "We were positive that he would come here first."

"Do you know Granny who owns that little restaurant downtown?" Before anyone could answer he returned to his story. "It seems that Jake hid for awhile, then this morning he broke into Granny's house. It's not far from the hospital so I guess he was going to steal her truck. Unfortunately for him Granny was home, visiting with the teenage girl who lives next door to her. He stupidly decided that he was going to take the teenage girl with him. Granny shot him with a double barrel shotgun, up close and personal."

"Holy shit. That must have been a mess," Matt laughed. "And just like her. She's one tough lady. After her husband died she moved into town and started that restaurant. We're actually related, shirt tail cousins."

At Bob's blank look, he explained, "You know, a cousin's cousin or a distant relative of a relative." At Bob's continued baffled look, he added, "It's a Southern thing I think. It makes the community related in some way to most people. And it makes all the people take care of each other." He shrugged, "We're related. I come from a large family so we have lots of those kind of kin."

"Well I'm an admirer of hers now," chuckled Deke. "She told Chief Smyth that she didn't mind Jake taking the truck, but when he started looking toward taking her young friend, she picked up the gun that was closest. Unfortunately for Jake it was that double-barrel. She's not even shook up, Smyth said. She's mad that he upset the young girl though," Deke laughed. "And made such an unholy mess."

"I love that old lady," Scott announced. "When I was a kid and Stella, my mom, forgot to feed me, she made sure that I had enough to eat. And then she'd give Stella hell," he grinned in remembrance. "If it hadn't been for Matt's dad, and that Granny I would have not survived nearly as well. It did teach me lessons though."

"Me and you Scott," admitted Deke. "I had parents similar to yours."

Bob kept silent. He couldn't even relate to the stories of the other men. His had been a quieter life with doting older parents of an only child. He had never wanted for anything until after they died. He had been allowed to paint or play whenever he wanted. He had never been abused in any way, not emotionally or physically.

In the upper middle-class neighborhood where he lived, he hadn't even known anyone who lived under dire conditions. There had probably been such people, but his mind had been focused on putting what was in his head onto paper or some other medium. He had been indulged and had taken it for granted.

No wonder Grandfather Youngblood had needed to come and give him a dose of reality of who and what he was and could be.

CHAPTER THIRTEEN

Lizzy was bouncing up and down in her seat by the time Leeann got into Kamon's truck. She heard a quiet, "Stop" coming from Kamon and a wide-eyed Lizzy immediately sat down. Expressionless, Kamon stared at Lizzy for a moment then returned to drive to the airport.

Lizzy now sat quietly looking out the window, seemingly undisturbed about being reprimanded.

"You have got to teach me how to do that," murmured Leeann just loud enough for him to hear. Surprisingly the intense man didn't intimidate her, maybe because he was much like Bob. She put her fingers to her lips, holding in the memory of the kiss they shared.

Kamon gave a slight smile but didn't reply.

As they drove through the gates of the airport, Leeann felt she had entered another world. In the last several weeks she had looked at documentaries on anything and everything. She thought she was prepared for a little airplane ride with a bumpy up and down flight as they drove to an almost deserted part of the Spring Creek airport. A helicopter sat on the airport tarmac.

"We're going in that?" She knew her voice trembled but her imagination didn't extend far enough to think about a helicopter.

"It's safe and allows for some flexibility," Kamon said softly. "This one is Sean's baby. Sean and Liam are twin cousins of ours, yours and mine." He carefully went through a check list of the helicopter, outside, then inside with its multiple dials.

Leeann said a silent prayer that he checked carefully.

Once in the air, the sight of the town, then the tops of the trees on the mountain replaced any residual fright with awe. She glanced back at Lizzy and Sammie. Lizzy was pointing out the window at something she wanted Sammie to see, seeming unafraid and interested in her new environment.

After a short flight, Leeann could feel the helicopter slow slightly as Kamon pointed out a meadow below. "Watch," he instructed looking out the window.

What had moments before been a grassy tree laden meadow was slowly moving to the sides of the area creating a long green airport runway. Leeann knew that her mouth hung open. It was magic. Absolutely magical.

"The runway is the brainchild of Liam and Sean McKinney. A long ago eccentric ancestor of ours named Jonathan Hicks flew B-12 bombers in World War Two. He built a hard-to-find runway cut into Sky Mountain," he pointed at the soaring peaks above them. "Each generation has added more technology to keep our Shadow Valley secret."

He slowly set the helicopter down on a green colored pad. "Catherine has requested all of us in Shadow Valley give you information about the things you see when you see them, so we don't overwhelm you all at once."

"Kamon, I'm overwhelmed already and we've just got here," she confessed smiling at the reticent man.

He gave her a rare slow smile. "Been there," he said softly.

The door was wrenched open by a large red-headed man with fading freckles and clear green eyes.

"Hi Leeann Ramsey, welcome. I'm Liam McKinney, a cousin of yours." He helped her down to the ground, she instinctively ducked to avoid the blades whirling overhead. Reaching into the backseat, he gently unbuckled Sammie. "Hi Sammie, I'm Liam. Let's get you out of there." He gently set Sammie on the ground, before he reached for Lizzie. "And I know you're Lizzie."

Wide-eyed, Lizzie suddenly developed a shyness, nodding her head. "Ok, now all of us will run over to that truck so I can take you up to the Stone House." Liam ducked his head, the children and Leeann following suit.

Kamon stayed in the helicopter listening to whatever was coming in on his headset. As they seated themselves in the truck, Liam excused himself for a moment to run back to talk to Kamon.

Leeann tried to take in everything around her, the large trees and bushes that now set like sentinels lined up on the edge of the meadow as if going into battle. The funny-looking very large half-barrel like structures with closed doors, but grass and shrubs growing on their rounded rooftops. The three of them watched with wonder as the trees and shrubs slowly returned to their places scattered in the meadow.

Leeann waved a thank you to Kamon who was still talking into the headset. He gave a slight lift of his hand in return.

Liam talked mostly to the children as they drove down a dirt road within what seemed like a thick forest of trees. Some of the trees were so massive that they completely block the sun from the roadway. Liam drove past several cottages built of cobblestone and wood. "I'm not going to explain who lives where right now. Eventually, you'll know all that."

Leann wasn't sure about that, but it was certainly all making her heart beat faster.

Liam drove around a bend in the road to stop before a huge house built of rough grey fieldstone.

The massive stone house was the biggest structure Leeann had ever seen. It looked to be at least three stories high and was backed up by soaring cliffs of the same gray-colored stone. Vines clung to the sides of the enormous building making it seem as if it had always been there, growing up from the ground. Huge oaks and hickory trees sheltered the roof.

"It's real," Leeann whispered. "Great-grandmother did pass on the truth. Her home was real. I thought it was just a story."

"Mama?" Lizzie's voice shook as she gazed upward.

"It's okay, baby," Leeann murmured. "Your great-great-grandmother lived here. We've come to visit new relatives."

"Is that a castle?" asked Lizzie. "It looks like one of those from that picture book of the fairy tale princess, except it's not quite as pretty."

"You're right it isn't as pretty," agreed Liam answering Lizzie. "Our ancestors built it more than a hundred years ago. They built it so it could be home for a lot of people if it was necessary for them to live there. Do you think we should go in and say hello?" he asked Lizzie with a serious tone, treating her as a young adult.

Lizzie nodded, "Sammie and I will hold hands so he doesn't get lost. It looks so big," she admitted.

"Good idea. If you want we can hold hands too," he added.

Liam helped the children up the wide slate steps to the wooden front doors of the house, Leeann following behind. The thick wooden double doors were twice as tall as she was and looked as ancient as they were.

"Are you sure this isn't a castle and that giants don't live here?" asked Lizzie to Liam.

"Yep. I'm sure. This is the headquarter home of our tribal clan. Your tribal clan, Lizzie. That means you belong here too. And the people here are your kinfolk."

"Please don't touch anything," Leeann reminded the children softly, intimidated by the sheer grandeur of the stone house.

Liam pushed an old doorbell, stepping back to listen to it ring, then opened the large door, holding it back for Leeann and the children to enter.

Two steps into the hallway and Leeann stopped. It was all there, just as she had been told by her mother who had been told by her mother.

The gigantic wrought-iron chandelier, held by a hand crafted chain, hung from the two storied ceiling timbers. Circular stone staircases were set on each side of the room leading up to higher floors. The deep red Persian rug stair runners were held in place by golden rods. Two walls were draped in embroidered banners, painting pictures of long-ago Scottish soldiers in battles. The third wall held swords with carved handles, old iron pikes and antique long rifles. Beautiful antique Persian rugs in faded jewel tones covered the stone floors. Several tables sat along the edges of the room displaying a collection of antique artifacts ranging from a small plated shield to porcelain figurines with inset jewels. The tall polished mahogany doors on each side of the entry were closed.

Liam indicated the door on the left side of the entryway. "Those doors lead down to another level. Our elected council, the Sgnoch Council, who make decisions for our tribal clan and their associates meet there. The rest of the downstairs is set up for emergencies with kitchens, beds and whatever Shadow Valley would need in case some sort of disaster or emergency."

Leeann blinked in wonder, her breath coming faster. "I remember bits and pieces of stories my mother and grandmother told me, but I honestly thought they were fantasies. Creative stories to keep me occupied."

Leeann felt tears prick the back of her eyes. Blinking them away, she struggled for composure. Thoughts of her great-grandmother flooded her heart and mind. Her poor great-grandmother had left this beautiful home to live in the backwoods. Leeann knew in her heart she had not left willingly but had been taken by force. No one would ever know the sorrow or pain her great-grandmother had gone through never to see her family, or home, or way of life again in her lifetime. Leeann blinked back tears for all their loss, especially for her great-grandmother's.

Liam led Leeann and the children down a long hallway lined with smooth cobblestones, Lizzie holding tightly to Sammie's hand.

Some doors to the hallway were open and some were

closed. In one open doorway, Leeann glimpsed a velvet sofa in front of a marble fireplace, in another an office with bookcases in back of a heavily carved wooden desk. There was a music room with a piano and some instruments she had never seen before. Another room seemed to be some sort of playroom with a wooden rocking horse with several low tables and chairs. Yet another room displayed an antique chess set on a carved table with chairs covered in brocade. Each room they passed seemed to have a different purpose.

Several halls jutted off from the wider one. Leeann could just imagine Lizzy, or worse yet Sammie, getting lost in the maze of halls and rooms. As the group followed Liam, the hallway became wider with textured wallpaper that shined like a silk handkerchief the store owner's wife had on display in North Fork. They stopped near what seemed like the back of the house.

Liam opened the door with a wide grin, letting Leeann and the children through first. The room was full of people. A huge banner with "Welcome Home" hung prominently from the chandelier to the room's edge.

A smiling Catherine came forward to take both Leeann's hands in her own. "I couldn't keep all these folks away. They were too excited to be able to meet you, and too glad that you're now here with us."

Leeann fought to hold back the tears threatening to overwhelm her. These were her people. Her mother's relations, and her own people. Losing the battle of tears, she smiled broadly at the people waiting to welcome her.

Catherine gave her a quick hug. "I'm not going to introduce you to all these people because you would never remember all their names. What is important is that all these people are related to you in one way or another. Either through blood or association."

She turned to the room and it became instantly quiet. "Everyone, I want you to meet Leeann Ramsey, her daughter

Elizabeth Ramsey, who everyone calls Lizzie, and this is Sammie." She smiled widely as she lay a hand on the little boy's shoulder.

Leeann was stunned. It was such an easy acceptance as if she had been a part of the group forever and had just come home. And was welcome as one of them.

"I'm a watering pot," Leeann told Catherine honestly, tears running uncheck down her face. "I feel so much that it's coming out of me in tears. Happy, grateful tears."

Catherine lifted her voice, "Leeann is going to have a lot of questions going forward. Answer all of them as best you can; as if I was asking them. She is part of us. Shadow Valley has secrets, but she needs to know who and what we are. No secrets from one of our own," she declared firmly. Several heads nodded in agreement.

The heavy silence was lifted as a little girl rushed up to Lizzie, "Hi Lizzie, my name is Alexandra but everyone calls me Alexa. You can call me Alex because we're going to be best friends, and Sammie's going to be too," she announced.

She held one hand out to Lizzy and the other to Sammie. "There's a playroom over in the edge of that corner," she pointed to a corner of the huge room. "It's gated and has a little fence around it because the babies, Claire and Anna, are crawling. We have lots of babies and little kids here. My daddy says there was a plethora of full moons. I don't know what that means. Do you?" she asked a bewildered looking Lizzie.

Lizzie shook her head, Sammie looking at Lizzie shook his too.

Alexa kept talking as she pulled Lizzy and Sammie toward the corner of the room. Several other small children followed them like baby ducklings going to the nearest pond.

Trent laughed as he gave Leeann a brief hug. "That's my girl, nothing like a little self confidence. I'd love to take the credit, but in truth she's just like her aunt."

"Hey," Raina objected as she and Kamon entered the room. "I'm her aunt too, but she is like Brenna. Let's differentiate between the aunts, please." She was holding the hands of identical twin, dark-haired little boys. Kamon followed holding identical twin auburn-haired baby girls, squirming to get down.

"Hey, Leeann. I'm so glad you're here," she said taking off the coats of the little boys as they struggled to follow the other children to the play area.

"Okay baby dolls, let me take you over to play," offered Joan, reaching for the twin girls, an older teenager beside her. "I'm Joan, Leeann, and this is my daughter, Thelma. I help Mrs. Searle here at the Stone House, but my husband Fergus and I live in the cobblestone gate house." Holding out her hands to the babies Kamon was carrying, she offered, "I'll take Claire and Anna over so they can watch the others play."

"Thanks Joan," both Kamon and Raina said in unison, then smiled warmly at each other.

"Claire and Anna?" questioned Leeann, stunned by the names.

"Anna was named for Anna Donovan, an ancestor of ours whose name I used when Sean and I went wanderin' to see the United States," explained Raina. "Claire was named after your great-grandmother, Anna Claire, whom I read about for years."

Leeann could only nod with wonder. Her connections to Shadow Valley was become stronger and less strange in the little time she had been here. She moved slowly around the room as people introduced themselves.

Leeann was taken unaware when a middle-aged woman gave her a warm hug. "I'm Alma MacPherson. This is my husband, Lachlan," she indicated a smiling elegant-looking gentleman. "I manage the pre-school and day care program with many helpers. Alexa has already informed me that she was bringing your daughter and Sammie to pre-school tomorrow."

"I'm so glad to meet you. Lizzie is bossy," Leeann admitted. "And Sammie doesn't talk."

"Then she and Alexa can rule the world of Shadow Valley together," Alma grinned. "Alexa has the confidence of Raina and the temper of Brenna, her aunts. Oh, tomorrow is going to be so much fun," she chuckled, then turned serious. "You know that they will have the best of care. We have lots of adult helpers, sometimes so many that it's an adult day care which the children and adults both love."

"I know you will," Leeann said, touching Alma's hand. "Brenna said you and the pre-school were outstanding."

Alma beamed, squeezing Leeann's hand again in affection.

An older woman with ebony skin, dressed in pale pink silk, stepped forward to introduce herself with a broad smile and a hug. "Welcome to Shadow Valley. I'm your Aunt Ulla," she said in a French-tinged accent. "I help with educational planning for all students and adults in Shadow Valley. Catherine has suggested that we meet in the mornings as she said you had many questions and want to learn everything."

"I'm grateful for your help," Leeann said honestly, intimidated by the beautifully dressed woman. "I know so little that I'm unsure what I don't know. If that makes sense."

"Oui, it does. Then say nine in the morning in the south breakfast room? Catherine and perhaps Raina may join us."

"That would be wonderful. Thank you. I'm grateful."

The rest of the afternoon was taken up with talking to the people of Shadow Valley and trying to remember who they were, and little details about them. She knew she would remember a few of them, but she promised herself that she would know each one of them soon. Her people. Her family and mostly kin. It was amazing to go from nothing and no one, to a community gathering of relatives. She felt like dancing, and crying, and giving thanks, emotions all tangled together.

Mrs. Searle, the housekeeper and general overseer, suggested that Leeann and the children might like to have a dinner tray sent to their room for the evening meal. Catherine and Raina would return to their own homes for the night as their children had to be put to bed.

Leeann agreed wholeheartedly. Lizzie became cranky and impatient when she was overtired. Sammie just laid down anywhere to rest without regard to place or overall comfort.

Mrs. Searle showed Lizzie to a small apartment with two connecting bedrooms and a Jack and Jill bathroom. The living area was done in shades of blue with a darker sofa and chairs. A small efficiency kitchen, microwave, and well-stocked refrigerator was in a large alcove, a children's play kitchen with dishes on the tiny table was in a nearby corner.

Mrs. Searle told her that if she needed anything to use the special phone and dial number four, which would go directly to her. She waved away Leeann's thanks saying, "We are all glad you are back home with us. We all want you to feel welcome. Catherine thought you might be comfortable in this tiny apartment near her office rather in an upstairs one. Later you can choose which ever one you wish for your permanent use."

Leeann thank her, silently smiling at what Mrs. Searle thought of as a small apartment. The contrast between her life now and several months ago was vast. She thought back to what her grandmother must have felt as she had gone from this beautiful place to the primitive backwoods country. It must have broken her heart.

After the excited Lizzy was put to bed, she held Sammie on her lap for cuddling while she read a bedtime story book aloud. She texted Bob that she was fine and would call tomorrow night. She was so tired, both emotionally and physically that she fell asleep immediately, waking only when she heard the rustling of bedcovers from the children's room.

CHAPTER FOURTEEN

The next morning Leeann dressed Lizzy and Sammie for pre-school, grateful for the clothes from Nurse Sarah. She had been told that Alexa would come and get them for school. Lizzy was fairly dancing with excitement by the time Alexa and Catherine arrived. Alexa announced that her daddy was downstairs and he was taking them to preschool that morning where they would have breakfast with the rest of the kids. Lizzy, and then a slow moving Sammie, gave Leeann a hug and a hurried goodbye as they followed Alexa out of the apartment.

"Sorry, Leeann, I know that Alexa is a whirlwind. Each day she becomes more like my sisters and her father. And Gabe is the spitting image of Trent in all ways. Please let the next baby be like me," she laughed half seriously. "They all can be overwhelming."

"You're pregnant?" Leeann asked breathlessly, glancing down at Catherine's flat stomach.

"Yes. But only the immediate family know."

At Leeann's frown she explained, "Brenna and Deke, Raina and Kamon, and you. You can tell Bob of course. Oh, I have to tell you that I have asked Bob not to visit for awhile to allow you time to assimilate into Shadow Valley. Texting or phoning is fine, but Bob is definitely distracting," she grinned, her eyes sparkling.

"Yes, he is," Leeann admitted, falling silent for a moment. "I can understand that," she said finally. "I need time for me. For me to figure out things here, and create a space for myself. Right?

Without a fine looking man distracting me," she giggled.

"Right. Thank goodness you understand. I was afraid you would think I overstepped and was too controlling. Which I am of course. It's part of being the elected leader of our matrilineal matriarchal tribal clan and associate clans."

"I'm grateful. In truth, I want to know more of who I am first. What I have the ability to learn and everything else I don't know. Does that make sense? I seem to be constantly groping for words to express feelings I've never had before."

Catherine smiled softly. "Yes it does. I had some of the same feelings when I met Trent."

"Oh I didn't mean that Bob ... he hasn't...," Leeann could feel the blush covering her face. "I meant that ...."

"You have time," Catherine murmured. "For now, let's go meet Aunt Ulla and Raina."

Late that evening, Raina and Kamon came to see her after she put the children to bed. Kamon spoke first, "We have news. Jake Downey broke into a house near the hospital with Granny and a young friend of hers in the house. Granny is a town matriarch and owns Granny's Café. Jake's plan was to steal Granny's truck, but also decided to take the teenage neighbor girl with him. Kamon grimaced, "Granny said she shot him with the gun that was handy, a double-barrel shotgun. Deke said it was up close and persona. An unholy mess."

"I'm sorry, Leeann, I was hoping that it would end peacefully," Raina inserted.

"Jake did not want to be taken alive. It sounds hard hearted, but he was not a good man in any way. The rumors that I heard when I was in school about him kept me terrified of ever being alone with him." Leeann gave a big sigh. "Now all the Downey's are dead. God have mercy on their souls."

"That pretty much says it all," Kamon said softly. "We wanted to tell you in person. Now we'll go and relieve Ione, our housekeeper, from being taken hostage by our little ones." His eyes were warm with affection as he put his arm around Raina to guide her from the room.

That night when Leeann and Bob talked they barely mentioned Jake or the Downey's. It was all in the past thankfully. They talked about their day with Leeann giving Bob an excited commentary of Shadow Valley, and the people she was meeting. She wanted to share all her enjoyment with him, wishing that he was physically there, but knowing that for now apart was best.

She loved being with him in whatever form that took. The several kisses they shared before she left made her heart sing whenever she thought about them, which was too often for her peace of mind. She had seldom been kissed and she had to admit that it was glorious, bringing intense feelings of excitement and the craving to touch every part of his body. And she wanted more. More kisses, and definitely more physical contact! She blushed as she thought of all the ways she wanted to please him.

Each morning for the next week, she met Aunt Ulla for coffee before they joined Catherine and Raina for breakfast. Aunt Ulla was sophisticated, worldly and completely tolerant of others foibles. Leeann quickly went from intimidation to awe to affection after the first meeting. Aunt Ulla treated her like she did Catherine and Raina, as a beloved niece.

Each day started with Aunt Ulla and Catherine asking Leeann what she wanted to learn that day. When she answered "everything'" they mapped out a daily schedule of things they felt she needed to know. Aunt Ulla or Raina were her teachers most of the time, but they also asked for outside help.

One day Sean McKinney spent the day teaching her the basics of the computer and the way the internet worked. Another day Mr. MacPherson invited her to his home to teach her business finances. She learned very little about business economics, but a lot about running a large household budget from both Mr. MacPherson and his wife Alma. Everyone she met was eager to assist in filling in the gaps in her education or to answer her multitude of questions.

Many of her days were spent in the huge Stone House library. The library was two stories high and held more books than Leeann could have imagined. The main floor held books from ceiling to floor, ranging from textbooks to novels to children's books. The middle of the library was covered with tables, chairs sitting on beautiful antique Persian rugs. Beveled window panes sat over window seats, half hidden by heavy drapes.

A circular staircase, unique in Leeann's experience, led to the upper area. The upper level ringed the lower room but housed older books, with smaller tables and chairs nearby. A leaded glass bookcase held the plain bound journal's of ancestor's.

For Leeann, the journals of her ancestors who had migrated to the United States was more interesting than any book could be. When Aunt Ulla found out that she was enthralled with the journals, she asked another cousin, Alex, a professor of Mythology, to show her the map the original group of ancestors had followed to the valley. Alex was Alex Ross, Dr. Alexander Ross, a large, ruddy faced gentleman of at least sixty. His salt and reddish hair was thinning on top and his blue eyes sparkled with good humor. He repeated and added to what Catherine had told her at Bob's house regarding their ancestor's history.

"Most people in the 1700's and 1800's migrated to either New York, the Carolina's, or Virginia, the middle of the eastern seaboard." He pointed to the large pull-down map with a laser. "There were well traveled shipping lanes from many of the European ports to the east coast of the United States so that way was fastest."

"Our ancestors chose to go down to New Orleans, Louisiana and travel up the Mississippi River to what is now Arkansas. As you know, New Orleans and the entire area was owned by the French. Our ancestor group were given a land grant from the

French King, and it was upheld by President Jefferson after the Louisiana Purchase. The Louisiana Purchase doubled the United States owned territory. Too much information?" he grinned.

"Nope. I didn't know any of that, or if I did, I didn't remember it."

Dr. Ross continued, "And you already know that immigrants from the European countries came for many different reasons. Some fleeing religious persecution, or wanting jobs, or freedom to become whatever they wanted to be."

"Our ancestors were fortunate to have a Seer who knew of the immense suffering coming to the Highlands of Scotland. You've read of the Jacobite uprising and the battle at Culloden and how Scotland was stripped of everything Scottish."

"I know the history," Leeann said softly, "what I don't understand is why?"

"Ah, the big question. Scotland and England had always fought over land and power. With Scotland on her knees after Culloden, it was an optimal time to strike the final blow to the power structure of the clans with cruel and bloody repression. With successful clan destruction, the Highland Chiefs lost their hereditary powers along with unique aspects of their lives, like of feudalism and the wearing of the tartan. And remember, Leeann, I'm relaying a Scots viewpoint, a very biased viewpoint. The English see it very differently."

"I'm unsure exactly what feudalism is," Leeann admitted.

"It was an economic, social, and political system where land that is owned by an Overlord is worked by peasant farmers. They owed the Overlord a portion of their crops and also worked in his fields. He provided housing, animals, and land to farm. The most important thing at that time in history was that he protected them from roving bands of robbers and foreign invaders. They weren't servants exactly, but sometimes damn close to it depending on the Overlord."

After she put the children to bed that night, she called Bob to tell him all the new knowledge she had learned that day. "Oh, Bob it's so exciting. Our tribal clan has a deep breathtaking history. With warriors, and intrigue, and battles. And such incredible hardships."

"You're reading the ancestors journals?" asked Bob, knowing the answer but wanting to hear her talk. Her range of knowledge was expanding rapidly, like building a brick wall one on top of the another very rapidly. And she was growing more self confident and stronger in spirit at the same time. He was so damn proud of her.

"Yes, and our ancestors were so courageous," she exclaimed.

"And Lizzie and Sammie?"

"Lizzie loves school, and loves Alexa, Catherine's daughter. Sammie spends a lot of time playing with the younger kids, even Russell and Robert, Raina's twins. Everyone here accepts both of them as they are, which is amazing to me. And Brenna was right, Lizzie's not so aggressive and her speech is better too. She copies everything Alexa does and both of them copy an older girl, Maggie. Lizzie says that Doug is Maggie's twin but they don't look alike at all."

"Ask Catherine to tell you their story." Bob changed the subject as clan law precluded him to talk about Maggie or anyone else. "And I can imagine Lizzie in school. She's going to be so smart. I miss the children, but mostly I miss you," he said softy.

"And I miss you too. There's so much I want to talk about with you, to share with you. And truthfully Bob, I don't know where the lines are."

"The lines? You mean like boundary lines? You mean what you can and cannot say to me? Those kinds of lines?"

"Yes," Leeann whispered softly. Finally, she was asking for what she wanted. What she needed to know. She was becoming who she was meant to be.

"Leeann, you can ask me anything you want, and say it any way you want. I'm here for you whatever it is. You've become very, very important to me. There is nothing that you have to hold back if you want to say it. Does that make sense? Or does that scare you silly?"

"It certainly doesn't scare me, except for the fact that I'm like a newborn and know so little about so much. But I realize I have no experience with male-female relationships, so I also don't want to get everything wrong and take too much for granted. I never had a boyfriend, or even a boy who was a friend. I feel completely out of my depth."

"Then we will take it slow. I will be whatever you want me to be. Your male friend, or more than that if that's what you want. Leeann, I want what's best for you whatever that is, but I hope that I'm in your life long term. Oh, one last thing Leeann. If you ever decide that you do want a boyfriend as you call it, I want to apply. First in line. And with that I'll say goodnight for now."

After they hung up the phone, Leeann sat quietly hugging herself. She might be able to have something she never had before; a mutual love relationship. Bob seemed to be saying that he could see them as a couple sometime in the future if she wanted it. Want it? Oh yeah. Thinking about the physical touching and loving made her blood flow faster, but the quiet times, just being with him, filled her heart to over flowing and gave her a soul serenity.

Catherine came to the door with Alexa the next morning. "You haven't had a chance to see the pre-school yet. I have to talk to Alma for a minute so I thought we could take the children to school today, if you wish."

"I'd like that. Lizzie is so excited each day that she can hardly wait for school to open."

"It has been good for her," Catherine murmured, "whether

142

you choose to stay here or go somewhere else, Lizzie probably needs school. And I think Sammie enjoys it too."

"I agree, but without the probably," laughed Leeann. The two women walked out of the house with the Lizzie and Alexa chattering away, Sammie walking beside Leeann holding her hand.

The preschool building had been revamped from a large storage shed and now was a first class educational play center. Leeann stopped in the large entry hall to look around at the small tables and chairs, low bookcases, mini kitchen sets, and cabinets. Scattered amongst the tiny furniture were large comfortable looking chairs and upholstered rocking chairs. Several parents, and elders milled about with the children, Raina and Kamon among them.

"Anna? Oh, my Anna," the quivering voice held anguish.

Catherine put her hand on Leeann's shoulder for support as they both turned to face an elderly man leaning on a silver cane, tears streaming down his deeply wrinkled face. The man must have once been very tall, but now was hunched over with age. Gray hair peeped from underneath a flat cap, tears seeping from the rummy old blue eyes as he examined Leeann's face.

A stunned Leeann stood silent as a gnarled veined hand reached out and touched her long multihued hair.

"You have to be my Anna's," the old man cried out, starting to slump forward on his cane. Before he could fall, Kamon and Raina were on each side of him, holding him erect.

"Let's go into Alma's office here and rest for a minute, Mr. Anderson," Kamon urged. "Raina, some water please." He settled the elderly man in a chair and sat closely beside him. He nodded, indicating to Leeann and Catherine to sit in the other chairs close to the old man who hadn't taken his eyes off Leeann.

Mr. Anderson sipped the water, closed his eyes for several moments, seemingly to pull himself together and asked, "Who are you? I know you're related to my Anna. No one on earth has that mix of auburn, gold and platinum hair except her."

Leeann was stunned and silent, not knowing what to do or what to say.

Kamon looked at Catherine, silently asking for permission to Mind Walk in this unique emotional moment.

Catherine nodded in acceptance.

"You knew Anna?" Kamon asked softly, knowing the history of the girl, Anna Clair Ramsey, who had disappeared without a trace years before. Raina had spent hours pouring over the details of the Grandmother Ramsey's young aunt's disappearance trying to find any clue to what happened to her.

"Anna was my JO.n, my sweetheart," he replied. "I looked for her for years, but she had been swallowed up by the earth it seemed. There was not the slightest trail. I finally had to accept that she was gone forever." Tears flowed freely down his face, mingling with the aged wrinkles.

"And that was before we had a satellite, or anyway to look for her except physically and mostly on foot," Kamon noted.

"I stayed in Shadow Valley for years afterward, hoping for any news, tramping over every inch of clan land. Nothing. She had disappeared into thin air. I never forgot, but I finally went to Falaichte, our island, to grieve. Later I moved to Skye and bought into a whiskey brewing company. I married late in life and lost my wife after ten years of marriage. I raised the kids, and helped the grandkids."

He stopped to take a breath, looking at Catherine. "I came back last year for the first time to discover Shadow Valley still felt like home. The other elders in the Childcare Center welcomed me. You know that Scotty Anderson is my youngest grandson."

Kamon nodded to Catherine that it was all true. He had felt the soul-shattering grief of Mr. Anderson as the man had searched for years for his lost loved one. And he had gone through the grief process, finally accepting that she was gone forevermore.

Silent tears were sliding down all three women's faces as they wept for all their losses, his, Anna's and all of Shadow Valley. And their history that had been changed.

Mr. Anderson gazed intently at Kamon. "I haven't officially met you, but I know that you are Kamon Youngblood, the Native American Mind Walker. I knew your grandfather well. And you know I speak true."

Kamon nodded and remained silent for several moments, then spread his hands in the age old sign of 'it's your call', whatever you decide, to tell the rest of the past or not.

The old man looked back at Leeann, slowly nodded in understanding. "You know that in mine and Anna's generation we married young and died young." He gave a long sigh, slowing the tears. "Anna and I were promised to each other. We had been everything to each other since childhood. We were marrying as soon as the priest could come." He stopped, closed his eyes, and swallowed.

Kamon placed his hands on the old man's hands, giving support in whatever the old man chose to divulge. Deep grief lurked just below the surface.

The old man continued, speaking softly directly to Leeann. "We were waiting for the priest, but were lovers before he could travel this far. Anna and I knew she was pregnant so we were excited and happy, even though we knew that the Council would not be. The day she disappeared ...," his voice choked. He started again, "That day I lost everything; Anna, the baby, and my own soul."

Leeann and Raina were openly sobbing while Catherine hugged both of them as tears flowed down her own face. The old man's grief was heartbreaking to hear, his world had been shattered in pieces around him.

"Could it ..., Do you think..., do you think that my grand-mother was that baby?" Raina asked hesitantly, her voice barely audible.

"Honestly, I don't know," the elderly man answered. He turned to Catherine as clan leader. "May I speak to Leeann alone please? I have many questions that are very personal, and I want to share my Anna with her before anyone else."

"Of course," Catherine agreed. "I have an important incoming call I have to take back at the Stone House. Raina? Kamon? Can you both stay?"

"Of course, Kamon and I will be here. We love to spend time with all the children. We'll be available if either of them need us," she replied to Catherine but was gazing at a smiling Kamon.

An hour and a half later, a beaming pair emerged from Alma's office. The old man immediately went to Kamon and Raina, "May I introduce you to my granddaughter, Leeann Ramsey," he announced softly. "We've figured out all the timelines of births and deaths. Leeann is my grand-daughter, but she was my Anna's great-grand-daughter since I married so late. We will DNA before we announce it publicly, with Catherine's permission of course."

"Now point out which ones are Elizabeth and Sammie, please. I want to just watch them for awhile before I walk over to the Stone House to make an appointment to meet with Catherine." The old man's face was alight with newfound happiness. He seemed to have become ten years younger.

"Oh and Raina. I do want both you and Kamon, Scotty and Nell, and Bob Neal to meet with us later." He grinned at Leeann, as she blushed deeply. He gave Leeann's hand a squeeze before he sat in a nearby chair to watch the children.

Leeann pulled Raina and then Kamon a quick hug. The three of them had become close friends over the last weeks. Raina was near her age and her sunny positive personality was similar to Leeann's own blossoming one. It was surprising, but she felt comfortable with Kamon too. Others were intimidated and awestruck by the intense man, but for her he was warm, introverted, and protective, much like Bob Neal. The couple had become her main support system in Shadow Valley.

As soon as she could, she needed to call Bob to tell him about the possibilities that might exist. There was also so much she wanted to share with him. She giggled to herself as she included some body parts.

CHAPTER FIFTEEN

"Oh Bob, the most wonderful thing has happened. I may have a grandfather still alive. Can you imagine? You may know him. He's Scotty Anderson's grandfather, which gives me a whole other line of cousins that I didn't know I had," Leeann gushed happily.

"Hey hey, sweetie, slow down. I can hardly understand you, you're talking so fast that it's getting jumbled for me. Now tell me what happened, please," Bob grinned at the sheer joy in Leeann's voice. "Tell me everything that's happened since last night when we talked."

Leeann jubilantly gave him a minute by minute account of all the things that had happened since early morning. "And Bob, he loved my great-grandmother so much that he spent years and years walking all over Shadow Valley looking for any trace of her. He told me that she was strong in spirit, and that laughter came easily to her. Oh, he told me how they had grown up together in Shadow Valley and that there had never been anyone else for either of them and that they were planning a wedding."

"And he said they knew she was pregnant when she was kidnapped. And they were both young but were really, really happy about the baby. And that she was walking from Stone House to the Anderson's farm when she was kidnapped."

"It was so sad, Bob. And he was so happy to have found me. And he's positive that I'm his Anna's great-granddaughter because my hair is just like hers and Lizzy's is the same ginger color as his used to be. And my grandmother's and mother's birthdays, they all fit." She stopped to take a deep breath. "Oh Bob, it's so good to belong. After mama died I didn't belong to anyone."

Bob's heart sank. He was so happy for Leeann, but knew that might be another impediment in their relationship. Going from an abusive relationship to zero family to two sets of intact loving families gave Leeann the safety net she needed. And she no longer needed him. If she chose him, it would be because she wanted him, rather than because of any need.

He swallowed hard as he said honestly, "Leeann, I'm so happy for you. Your identity is now known. Not only do you have the Ramsey clan with all the far flung cousins, but you may also now have all the Anderson's and their people. And Lizzie and Sammie will have that safety net of family too."

"Bob, I feel as if somehow I'm living in a dream world. This can't happen to me. Everything is occurring so fast. And changing. I have to go now as Mr. Anderson wants to see me after he meets with Catherine which he's doing right now."

"That's fine, Leeann. I hope it's good news for you," he said trying to keep the smile in his voice. "I'm here whenever you want to talk."

Inside his heart was breaking at the loss of the possibilities. Leeann had moved on. She had found family and made new friends. He could hear the happiness and sheer elation in her light laughter. And he was truly glad for her. He wanted her to be happy. He had hoped that her life would be intertwined with his, but it seems that was not to be.

For him, Leeann was like a fledgling swan, unsure and inexperienced but with the potential to develop into a strong beautiful creature. And she was growing and gaining so much self confidence that it was breathtaking. He now had to recognize that her life's journey might not be his, but if she ever needed anything he would be there for her. Whatever that path took.

Leeann slowly hung up the phone. Bob sounded odd to her. In all the time they had talked a certain tone of voice had been present. Caring, loving, and kind of flirty. Now it wasn't there.

Had the distance between them made him change toward her? He was so strong, mature and incredibly handsome, and as Louise would say, out of her league.

Bob walked toward the front porch so deep in thought that he almost missed the house phone ringing. He hurried inside to answer it.

"Bob, this is Catherine."

"Hey Catherine, Leeann just called me to tell me her good news, she may have a great- grandfather still alive."

"Actually, it's probably a grandfather on the Anderson's side, but a great grandmother on her mother's side as her family seemed to have married really young. I'm not sure exactly how that works. Which brings me to what I called to ask."

Bob held his breath. Catherine was the leader of the clan, essentially the Chief person of the matrilineal matriarchal tribal clan. Whatever she asked, he would grant. The continuation of Clans under her banner thrived because of the order of the ancient laws. Laws which gave the people the right to elect a clan leader, and then abide by the decisions made.

"I'm willing to do whatever you need," Bob answered honestly. "Whatever that is."

"Well we don't need a telephone, our moccasin telegraph works better," Catherine complained. "Somehow word got out that Leeann is a Ramsey, a young beauty, and has all the financial assets of the family. So far it is not known that she may also be Mr. Anderson's granddaughter."

"Isn't that a good thing? Leeann has a family. Something she needed and never had in the situation she was in," Bob stated, perplexed by Catherine's lack of enthusiasm.

"Not from my point of view it isn't. We are going to be overwhelmed with suitors for Leeann's hand, to put it in an old fashioned way. Leeann has no experience in handling men, especially sophisticated Scottish men. Add to that forceful Scots

150

with our Native American blood lines. It gives me a headache just thinking about it."

"Holy hell," Bob breathed softly. He had not thought of that. Of course, men would be falling over each other for a marriage with Leeann Ramsey. She was the whole package; young, beautiful, rich, and with impeccable bloodlines. As an added bonus she was part of two powerful clans.

"That about sums it up. Normally, I would send her to Falaichte, our island, but she would be in the same situation there. Same thing in Paris, with Marie's daughter, or with the Durie's in Canada. All those place are available to some tribal clan members."

Bob was silent as he absorbed the problem. "So you obviously have a solution, something I can help with."

"I can do what Brenna did with the measles when she quarantined you. I can put out the word, a quarantine, that Shadow Valley is off limits for everyone until the situation with Leeann and an Associate clan is resolved."

"The Associate clan being the Anderson's?" Bob queried. "That makes sense. It will also give Leeann a chance to check out the options that are available to her. How can I help?"

"You do know that her options are many," Catherine reiterated. "However, Brenna, Raina and I felt that you were interested in Leeann as perhaps a permanent joining. Is that not true?"

"You do want your pint of blood, my cousin, don't you? The answer is yes; I am interested in a forevermore relationship. Until she actually left here, I didn't know if how serious it was for me, so much was happening all at once, especially with the Downey's. And quite frankly, it was much easier to deny my own feelings rather than accept what is. Now I want to follow the edits of clan law and permanently join our lives."

Catherine started to speak but Bob interrupted. "Please let me finish Catherine because you need to know. First and foremost, Leeann chooses. I want Leeann to be happy, whatever that takes. She deserves every ounce of happiness that can be had in this world. That's my primary goal. And if she chooses another path that is not mine, then I will live with it. Destiny."

"Secondly, Catherine, I am more like Kamon than even I recognized before Leeann came into my life. I am too intense, too driven, and too focused. I overwhelm even myself sometimes. I'm a selfish bastard who has wanted it all. I don't know if that's possible for me."

"Are you finished describing someone that I know? I know both you and Kamon exceedingly well, both as the tribal clan leader and by experience as I've observed both of you. You're right in that you are very much alike. And Bob, with a few adjustments in your life, you can have it all. As Kamon does."

Bob started to speak, "But ...."

"And please do not interrupt me again," Catherine insisted in a stern voice. "For now, this is the situation. No one knows if Leeann will choose another mate or not. There is no reason she should unless she desires it. She was badly abused the first time around with Leroy Downing so that she may chose to remain single. And if she determines that the single path is what she wants, she is going to need a bodyguard. Ramsey women must have a guardian from the Warrior Society if she decides to live or even travel off of clan lands." Catherine fell silent, letting Bob absorb the information.

Catherine continued in a softer voice. "We don't know how strong the Ramsey women's blood flows through Leeann's veins. She could be like Brenna, Raina, and I where there would be a significant blending of abilities whether the match was forced or not. Or she may have none of the ability to share any aptitudes."

"I'm sorry Catherine, but I do not understand the blending part. I probably should but I don't."

"This part of our history only involves Ramsey women and their offspring, so you never had the need to know. With the exception of the Sgnoch Council, few others are aware of this aspect of our heritage."

"Brenna, Raina, and I are direct descendants of the original woman-child of our ancestors as is Leeann. Each female Ramsey has been protected by the Warrior Society, a byproduct of the Sword and Shields promise of the ancient clans and forevermore honored."

"As you know, if a Ramsey female is mated by force she is bonded to that person for life, and can never have a child with him. What few people know is that they will have a blend of their gifts or abilities. If the Ramsey female chooses her mate then there is a stronger exchange of abilities, and then a child is possible," Catherine explained. "Because of the kidnapping of her great-grandmother we have no idea what the future holds for Leeann. She may, or may not, bond with a mate. And may, or may not, be able to have another child. And the blending of abilities or gifts could be very powerful or not at all. Of course, I cannot See her future either which makes the situation doubly difficult. And you know Bob, I cannot see your future either."

Bob spoke slowly, thinking it through, "Leeann did not choose Leroy Downing and she had a child, so it's entirely possible that she may not be able to conceive again?"

"Right. But back to the original subject, it is the birthright of Ramsey women to have a Warrior to protect them. Bottom line Bob, are you interested in becoming Leeann's bodyguard? I know you went through the training when you were in college. It would mean a three or four-week refresher course in Scotland."

She took a deep breath and continued, "Take some time to think it over and I'll call you in a couple of days," Catherine suggested.

"No need, Catherine. Yes. I wish to petition you and the Sgnoch Council for permission to serve as Leeann's bodyguard. You know that I will protect her with my life."

"And your art? You are very gifted, as you well know. Protecting Leeann will unquestionably cut into your time and focus. And there is the added responsibility of Lizzie and Sammie. I had to think over all the aspects before asking you first," Catherine admitted. "Your artistic gift will be secondary to what Leeann wants and chooses. Be very very sure before you make that commitment. She will be first, you will be second."

"Leeann is first now, in my heart and in my head. My art is not as important to me as Leeann's well being. I've only recently been able to recapture my artistic feelings on paper. If I will no longer have that capability, it's a cheap price to pay for Leeann's safety and happiness, and I'll gladly pay that price."

"Done," stated Catherine. "Be at the Spring Creek Airport in an hour, either Liam or Sean will pick you up and fly you to Scotland. Arrangements for your return will be made by the Scotland group. Please do not call Leeann and inform her of this decision. I will inform her that you won't be able to talk with her for several weeks as you're doing something for me. Good Luck." The phone clicked off.

Bob looked down at the dead phone. In fifteen minutes his life had taken another turn. The Warrior Society. It was the hardest, most concentrated physical and mental training he had ever done.

Originating in the 1700's after Culloden, all the centuries of fearless, violent strategies of warfare had been modernized with new weapons and techniques into a warrior society. This while keeping the honor of the clans intact, and functioning within ancient tribal clan law.

Kamon had said that the Warrior Society leaders had taken their warlike past, mixed it with all the US Navy Seals training manual, put it all on steroids, and added a level of psychological combat with a touch of sadism. Bob totally agreed with that description.

Good grief, he was still standing on the front porch and

one of the twins would be there in 14 minutes. He quickly called Hank who was working in the barn. He told him that he had an important meeting that he had to attend and would be gone for three weeks or four weeks. Hank simply asked if he wanted him to do anything special. Bob gave him free rein and told him that if there was anything important that he couldn't decide to call Deke and Brenna.

His next phone call was to Deke to ask him to make whatever decision that couldn't wait until he returned from the Highlands.

"Brenna just told me that you are headed to Scotland for a refresher course of the Warrior Society," Deke stated with laughter in his voice. "I honestly didn't know that I could hurt so much in body parts I didn't know could be hurt."

"Yeah, I remember too well. And I needed a reminder of that now because ....?" Bob grinned in spite of his own painful memories of the physical aches he knew was coming.

"I remember being you. I thought I was in great physical shape, then I became acquainted with MacLennan and Buchannan and some others. When do you leave? Do you need a lift to the airport?"

"No, but thanks. I'm packing as we speak. If Hank needs anything though, please do whatever you think is best. And thanks Deke."

Bob quickly finished packing older rough clothes with good sturdy shoes and boots. He threw in a swimsuit, grimacing at the thought of the ice-cold mountain streams and the lakes they poured into, the very lakes, or lochs as the Scots called them, that he knew would be part of the swimming instruction. He detoured through the kitchen to explain his leaving to Louise and found that Hank was there filling Louise in on the news. They both looked exactly like they were; sparkling happy newlyweds sharing warm glances and secret smiles.

The trip to Scotland was easy and fast with Liam as pilot

and Sean as co-pilot. The twins were trying out a new jet fuel which didn't surprise Bob at all, but was incredibly boring to listen to all the meticulous scientific details. He slept for most of the trip.

In Scotland, Bob was met by Murdock MacLennan, Master of the Warrior Society School. He explained that he would be turning over the first part of Bob's physical retraining to Patrick Buchannan. If it wouldn't have made him sound like a weakling, he would have groaned out loud. Patrick Buchannan was a middle-aged man of average height, with a thick muscular chest and powerful limbs. And he was a legend.

For the next two weeks, Bob spent every moment, awake and asleep, in training alongside Buchannan. He spent each day in a variety of physical activities from pushup, to running on rough terrain, to hand to hand combat drills without weapons. His nights were spent sleeping on a forest floor, rolled up in the McNeil tartan of black and muted blue with the yellow and white stripes.

Each day he pushed himself to a level where his muscles and mind screamed in protest. And each time he stopped, Patrick Buchannan continued the exercise, silently showing Bob how much further he had to go to reach his own limits. Bob found that the silent Buchannan deserved every ounce of his superstar reputation.

Older now, Bob had thought that his body was in better than average condition until the Warrior Society retraining started. Grandfather Youngblood had insisted that he spend at least an hour a day of maintaining his body's strength. His home gym helped, but the range of abilities Patrick Buchannan lead were far beyond his own personal training regimen.

He had always been excellent with a rifle or handgun, although did not surpass Buchannan. He was taller and loved running, but he also did not exceed him in running to the tops of the steep hilly crag's. Swimming in the ice cold stream however, was the only event where he actually exceeded his mentor. It seemed that Buchannan hated the icy water coming directly from the snow covered mountains.

Bob lost track of the days, as he sought to become the best Warrior he could be. He pushed the limits of his ability, trying to make each day better than the one before it. His arms and legs ached along with every other muscle he didn't know he had.

Grandfather had told him that the physical pain in training was a reminder of your role as a guardian. Your very life was on the line to protect. The sacred oath.

He had been trained by the Warrior Society previously in martial arts, but it had been several years since he had used the training consistently. He was given a short refresher course to relearn how to most effectively use the stiletto to silently kill with a minimum of blood spilled. The long thin stiletto used was double sided, honed to razor sharpness, and was very efficient in close body contact. He only had to spend a little time in the anatomy course as his mind consistently used body images in paintings.

It had taken nearly three weeks before Bob was able to feel that he could guard against all comers and win. He finally earned a "s math a rinn thu" from the silent Patrick Buchannan, he knew enough of Scottish Gaelic to translate as "well done". Since Patrick Buchannan was from the lowlands of Scotland, Scottish Gaelic was the most common language between them.

Then he had been turned back over to Murdock MacLennan. "Patrick tells me that you are physically capable of guardian status, especially proficient with a knife."

"The only problem I had with Patrick was he's damn good in everything. He didn't break a sweat when my own muscles screamed. And he's probably a good fifteen years older than I am," Bob chuckled ruefully.

"Yes, he is. Now for the last week, we will be dealing more with the historical and psychological parts of the Warrior Society. This will be a quick review as I'm sure you've been told all this before. Of course we will do a minimum of physical training. Mostly running to the top of that peak over there each day and back to keep you in shape, and a few rounds of hand to hand combat, mostly to keep *me* in shape," MacLennan grinned. "Patrick says you are a worthy opponent which is high praise indeed."

Bob knew that the history of Scottish fighting was based on the premise of ferocious combat, swift reaction time, and superb physical conditioning. His own clan, the MacNeil's, motto was *Buaidh no bas*, 'to conquer or die'. The MacNeil's had fought with the Jacobite's at Killiecrankie and later at Culloden. They paid for being on the losing side with exile and imprisonment, but were not required to forfeit their estates. Even in the present day, the MacNeil's divided their time between the United States and Scotland.

MacLennan continued, "The greater part of being a Warrior is in your mind, not in the physical challenges of your body. Your role is to be a guardian, not a soldier. To protect. You know that to protect sometimes its necessary to defend with force. For the next few days you will get a refresher course of the history of the Celtic Warriors from which our Society originated."

And review he did. Each generation had left a plethora of skill sets for the next generation to follow. From the earliest Celts, to the Celtic Warriors as for-hire mercenaries, onto the remnants of the societies in Scotland, Wales and Ireland. Like building blocks each ancestor group contributed to the next generations rigorous teaching. Bob was reminded of the culture from which he had come. The history of the fierce war-like nature of the Celtics and their courage in taking on all comers from Romans to Englishmen. He paid homage in his heart to the courage of Scotland, assessed the long road traveled, and was reminded that courage is not an innate ability, but rather it is a chance to serve. To act as Sword and Shield.

On the day he was to leave, Patrick Buchannan, Murdock MacLennan and four other men presented him with a short double-sided stiletto with ornate carvings on the silver hilt.

Placing the flat of the knife in his palm, Murdock held

the hilt toward Bob. "You are as you were destined to be. You have conquered all challenges and have the honor and integrity within as a member of the Warrior Society. You have already taken the blood oath of secrecy. You have chosen to place another's well-being above your own. You are worthy." Murdock placed the hilt of the stiletto in Bob's hands, bowed from the waist, and stepped back.

"Thank you, I am honored," Bob said sincerely. "You have retrained me to serve in whatever capacity is my Destiny. I am in your debt forevermore as I fulfill the duties assigned to me," he said formally, bowing his head.

Each man raised his dagger above his head as they formed a circle and repeated the ancient vow together.

"In secrecy we swear to protect you and yours forevermore. We will always be your Sword and Shield; we swear with honor. Let death be the judgment of any man or woman who speaks of this event of today. Today will forever be shrouded in secrecy as our own beginnings are shrouded."

CHAPTER SIXTEEN

Leeann was engrossed in learning the complicated system of governing Shadow Valley from clan membership, elections of leaders, and the edits of ancient law. Catherine and Raina were usually her teachers, but everyone in the valley was willing to assist her in learning each facet she needed to know.

The DNA results came back were proof positive she was John Anderson's grand-daughter. All of the Anderson's welcomed her, a large reception would be given when Catherine deemed it appropriate.

Mary O'Riley, Catherine's financial wizard and emissary traveling outside the valley, sat her down and explained how the finances of the tribal clan worked. How money invested by each generation was paid in quarterly revenues to each tribal clan member, but if there was a greater need, then other arrangements could be made.

"Then if there's no need for earning money, what do all these people do?" questioned Leeann, distressed. "Mary, I could never just sit on my hinny."

Mary patted her on the arm. "That's not how it works here. This tribal clan have ancient rules of ethics and morals that each person must contribute whatever they are able; whether it be in service, or any other talent or gift they have been given. But we have the freedom to decide what is right for us. What you must do, Leeann, is to be of value. To serve. To become the strongest most you can be."

Mary had gone on to tell her that her grandfather Anderson had settled a lump sum of money on her to access immediately. She also indicated that she would receive quarterly monies from the Ramsey clan as they all did.

Dr. Ross helped her in her search for any information on any subject that she wanted to know. All she had to do was ask. He seemed delighted to guide her in whatever direction she wanted. He treated her as a younger equal, mentoring without pandering.

"That's really interesting," murmured Leeann to herself, not realizing that her voice had carried to the university professor. Leeann was sitting in a window seat in the massive Shadow Valley library, a place she could often be found when Lizzie and Sammie were in preschool.

"What have you found?' asked the smiling middle-aged man, rising to his feet to join her. He had told Catherine in front of her that he was delighted to mentor such an inquiring student, one who was thirsty for new knowledge. Leeann was always unsure of her own intellect so Dr. Ross's words were like warm honey poured over her.

"I found a book on ancient Celtic Warriors. Yesterday I read about Native American in their early days. I'm struck by how similar their beliefs and attitudes were, and I'm so sorry I interrupted you."

"You're reading is much more interesting than the research I'm doing for a new book on Greek Mythology. What do you find similar, or along the same lines?"

"First I have to tell you that I followed everything you said about checking the sources of books to be sure that the past history is valid, reliable and well-researched. This one is."

"Excellent. If it's one man's opinion, that is fine as long as you know that and don't base a thesis on it," he grinned. "Your opinion might be better than his or her opinion."

Leeann smiled broadly at the middle-age man. He had become a dear friend as he kept asking questions until he gently steered her toward figuring out the answer for herself.

"There's literally dozens of things that are similar. For example, neither group allowed themselves to be lazy. They subsisted mostly on meat which they ate with their hands sitting on the ground or floor. In later generations, their older children served them at the table. A Native American leader was only a leader as long as he had people following him. When they no longer wished to follow him they either left, or chose a new leader. For the Celts, a village leader or chosen Chieftain settled disputes, same as the Native American. In both cultures, young people often learned to be a warrior by doing solo raids or with peers. Oh, and women were often in leadership positions like medicine women, and respected by both cultures."

"Interesting," Dr. Ross replied. "Anything else?"

"For me it is amazing that the Celtic druids and the Native America medicine man or woman spiritual leaders are so similar. They both believed in Father Sun and Mother Earth, both were supposed to boast of their battle feats, and both had mystical ancestors with special gifts."

"That's exciting, Leeann. I knew some of that but not all. The legends say Druids were highly intelligent, some of them could Mind Walk, and predict the future." His eyes twinkling, he asked, "Hmm, now who do we know who have similar gifts from the Creator?"

"Mama, can I come in? I need to talk to you," Lizzy's voice was soft and hesitant as she interrupted.

"Of course, Lizzie, please do."

Lizzie waved a greeting to Dr. Ross as he went back to his table to give the mother and daughter some privacy. She held Sammie's hand as she took several steps into the library. "Sammie feels hot," Lizzie informed her mother.

Leeann immediately erased everything else from her mind,

placing her hand on Sammie's forehead in the universal mom movement of checking a child's temperature. He did feel warm and his skin was a little moist.

Sammie had so many medical problems from congenital defects to early birth weight. She had researched on the little magic computer box that 15% of all Down Syndrome childhood deaths in 2017 was from pneumonia and other respiratory diseases. Combine that with the congenital defects and low birth weight made Leeann play hover-mother at Sammie's slightest sniffle now.

When she had lived in the backcountry, survival was her primary concern. Now armed with new knowledge of the seriousness of Sammie's health problems, she had turned into an over-protective parent. She had already called Brenna twice since coming to Shadow Valley with questions, so she would take his temperature first before bothering her again.

Brenna's clinic building, set immediately behind the house, was always open even if no one was around. She quickly found a thermometer, choosing a digital easy read one and placed it gently under Sammie's armpit. He hates anything near his ears and taking a rectal temp was not easy either. After three minutes the digital thermometer dinged and she was able to read it. Normal.

After breathing a sigh of relief, she asked Lizzie, "What were you and Sammie doing just before he got hot?"

"We was 'arunning from the back porch to the garden fence. Whoever was fastest gots to pick the trucks we were using to haul the dolls."

"Who was playing this running game?" Leeann asked gently.

"Alexa, me, and Sammie." Lizzie frowned in dismay, "Oh I see. Sammie was hot from the running. I shoud'da thought of that."

"Yes, and remember Sammie runs slower and its harder for him which is not his fault. Do you think that game was a fair way to decide who got to chose?"

Lizzie scrunched up in nose and forehead in thought. "Nope, it wasn't." Turning to Sammie she gave him a hug and an apology.

"Mama, can I ask you something else? It's sort of important to me."

"Lizzie you can ask me anything, important or not," she assured the little girl.

"You know my cousin Maggie, who's like nine or ten?" Not waiting for an answer in typically Lizzie fashion, she continued, "Of course you know her. Anyway, she said that when I grow up and I'm a big person, that I'm going to be a famous writer. And mama, I can't even read. Well, I can read a little, but not good," she said honestly. "So how does Maggie know that?"

Leeann had asked and had been told by Catherine that young Maggie would become a psychic in adulthood. No one knew what form that would take, or how strong her abilities would be. She mostly stayed in Shadow Valley and was protected by everyone there. Douglas was Maggie's constant companion. Both orphans, the two had been born the same day from different parents in different parts of the world, but insisted they were twins. Catherine had also told her that Raina's twin baby girls were gifted. And the three girls were the only gifted people in the Shadow Valley.

Good grief, asked Leeann to herself. *How do you explain a Maggie to a four-year-old when it was a difficult concept for adults to grasp?* She answered her own question in her head. *You give them the simplest explanation that they can understand, and what is most important to them.*

"Then maybe you better learn to read better, and to use better grammar. What do you think?" Leeann questioned.

"Yep, you're right. I'm going to do that. C'mon Sammie, lets go outside to play, but you have to walk slow," she instructed, taking his hand and walking slowly beside him.

Leeann returned to her suite of rooms in the Stone House, feeling restless and unsettled. After pacing, sitting for a few moments, picking up a book and putting it down, she drifted over to the window, looking out at the expansive valley.

Through the window she could see the afternoon shadows playing light to dark games along the back lawns. Huge oak trees with their hundreds year old bark and massive branches protected like giant leafy umbrellas. Shadow Valley with Sky Mountain in the background was a visual feast of greens, each landscape vying for first place. The peace and serenity of the mountains seemed to drift into the valley creating a tranquility for its residents.

She loved Shadow Valley, and all its people. She was beginning to form a strong bond with her grandfather and her girl cousins were the best friends she had ever known. She shut her eyes, letting her mind drift, and tried to imagine her mother's long ago voice. She could only remember one thing from her mother's which would apply to her situation now, "Your Destiny is written, but the details are all yours to make."

Instead of the contentment others seemed to show, Leeann was restless and uneasy. She knew that she was safe which had been a constant worry throughout most of her life. She knew that she was loved and belonged to this wonderful family.

Lizzie was learning and growing each day and Sammie was happy and healthy. Then why wasn't she ecstatically happy? She should have been dancing to have the life she had now. Instead she was melancholy and cheerless. Her morose musing was interrupted by a knock on the frame of the open door.

"May I come in?" Raina asked.

"Please do, my own company is driving me crazy," Leeann admitted.

Raina grinned at the unusual frown on her cousins face. "Then I'm glad that I saw you coming from the clinic. Is everything all right?"

"Lizzie was concerned about Sammie being hot, but it was from running to keep up with her and Alexa rather than a temperature from sickness."

"That's so sweet," Raina gushed. "She watches out for Sammie in so many ways. Now tell me why the long face. What's wrong and how can I help?"

"I'm going through some sort of phase that I hate, and I don't have a clue as to why," confessed Leeann grimacing at her thoughts. "I'm an ungrateful wretch, as Dr. Ross would put it."

"Well your life has certainly changed in a very short time," declared a smiling Raina. "Do you think it's just that so much has happened that it's stressful? Would you like to talk about it?"

"Yes, please. Maybe a little is stress but ...," Leeann very softly. "I'm going to sound like I'm a combination of crazy and unappreciative."

She took a deep breath and blew it out slowly. "I love all of you, my new Ramsey sisters, my new grandfather Anderson, and all the cousins. Shadow Valley, the Stone House, and all its inhabitants have been wonderful for me but ...," she stopped.

Raina remained silent, letting Leeann work the problem through.

A long couple of minutes passed before she added, "Raina, I think I need more."

Again Raina stayed silent for several moments, knowing that Leeann would finish the thought in her own time.

"I need to be needed I think," Leeann said softly. "I need to contribute," her voice sounding stronger and less hesitant. "I need to have my own kitchen even if its tiny, to cook my own food. Oh Raina, that all sounds so silly when I say it aloud."

"Actually, it doesn't, and you do know that I cannot lie."

"Here in Shadow Valley nothing is required of me. I could sit on my hinny all day if I wanted. Or study the mating habits of red beetles in the massive library. I could do literally anything I desired. But what I really want is a home, to raise the kids as best as I know how, maybe even have a husband to love, and more kids someday."

"That makes sense to me. I think we all have to come to terms with the dichotomy of each of us – what we want with who we are. The fork in the road."

"What should I do?" questioned Leeann.

"Leeann, you've only told me in the vaguest of terms what you want," chuckled Raina. "Do you have any specifics?" At the deep blush on Leeann's face she laughed aloud. "Oh, yeah you do."

"Raina, I love Shadow Valley but I think I want to be a visitor, not a resident. There I said it and it's a completely selfish act on my part. Lizzie and Sammie love it here with new friends, family, and preschool. I have it all and I'm dissatisfied. That makes me a terrible person," she frowned, unhappy with herself.

"No, it makes you an individual human. It makes you part of humanity, striving to be who and what you are. Leeann, that's not a bad thing. We all do that when we move forward in life."

Taking Leeann's hands in both of hers she added, "Leeann, we will remain your family, through the good times and bad times. We're here for you, just like if we had a need you would be there for us. And we're not going anywhere. Families are a permanent situation. You are a Ramsey. Leeann Ramsey, and a grand-daughter in the Anderson clan. That is who you are. That can't be changed. But Leeann, that doesn't define you as a human being."

Leeann stared wide-eyed at her closest female friend.

"You have talents, and needs far beyond who you come from. We all do. I needed my connection to Kamon Youngblood in whatever form that took. He completed who I was and what I wanted to be. He still encourages me to fulfill any part of me that I want to pursue. I need that boost to try new things and to keep being me. He's a strong personality in his own right, but that doesn't swallow up who I am, if that makes sense."

Leeann nodded in thought.

"For Catherine, it was accepting that her gift of Second Sight was an integral part of her very being. She had to acknowledge that she wouldn't even change it if she could. She had to accept the core of her being before she found her happiness with Trent. Does that make sense to you?"

"In a strange way it's very helpful. You're giving me permission to be me as I am; a woman raised in the backwoods, with a few talents, a just-found loving family, and a future I chose. Right?"

"Yep, that's it," Raina smiled at Leeann's quick understand. "And that choice does not have to mean you live in Shadow Valley. Or Spring Creek, but that you can chose wherever you want to go. Brenna decided that for her and her family she wanted to live outside the valley but remain a deeply connected part of it. She and Deke thought that was the best for them as a couple. That may, or may not change in the future."

"That takes my breath away," Leeann said honestly. "Raina, you are a balm to my soul. You have answers when I didn't even know the questions to ask."

"Nay, I'm just a little bit older than you," Raina laughed. "Our paths must have mingled a hundred times before we met. You are the sister of my heart. Having you in my life adds to my own contentment."

"Now what are we going do and may I help?" Raina giggled in anticipated delight.

CHAPTER SEVENTEEN

Bob was finally home. It had surprised him that Kamon chose to fly to the Falaichte, the private clan island, to pick him up in the little Lear jet, Liam as co-pilot. The last three plus weeks had been physically exhausting. Now the safe haven of going home in the company of cousins gave him a letdown after all the adrenalin flowing through in his veins. He settled in the comfortable seat, put up the leg-rest and in seconds was sound asleep. Hours later, he woke up to hear the engine slowing as they dropped into the flight pattern of Spring Creek.

"You were not a wonderful companion," teased Liam. "All of your verbal response were snores and snorts."

"I'm sorry, guys. I have never been so drained in my life. The second time around was not any easier than the first time I went through the training. Days training and nights on the cold hard ground wrapped in my plaid. The only time it wasn't so bad was the last three days re-learning the history of the Swords and Shields, plus a major part of Scotland history. In those few days, we only ran about ten miles a day to the top of a hill. My toenails are even exhausted."

"Oh, I remember that," Liam admitted. "I'm glad I was a lot younger when Catherine sent me and Sean."

"Agreed," said the grinning Kamon. "Oh, there's Deke to pick you up, we gave him a call while you were sleeping."

Deke got out of his truck, tossed Bob's duffel bag in the back, and waved to the little Lear as it took off back toward

Shadow Valley and the hidden Sanhicks Airport.

Bob and Deke discussed the difficulties of the various physical exercises that the Warrior Society required. Both of them felt that the training with the thin stiletto knife was the hardest. With the knowledge of the bodies anatomy, the double edged knife could kill instantly, leaving almost no blood or sound. They had each been awarded the carved possession at their ceremony as the six men raised their daggers above their head to form a circle. The new initiate placed his knife as the seventh man and each repeated the ancient vow, the new initiate repeating the sacred vow last.

As he neared his home, Bob vowed his allegiance silently to the woman he had sworn to protect with the ancestor's warriors code if that was his destiny.

Deke pulled up to the house, Bob retrieved his duffel from the back of the truck and thanked him. Deke gave a grin and a jaunty wave as he drove off down the driveway.

Bob stood for a moment admiring the silent house. It looked good. He started forward as the door burst open spilling out Lizzie, a silent Sammie, Leeann, and an elderly gentleman, all yelling "Surprise".

"I thought you were never gonna come home," Lizzie yelled, leaping from the porch to wrap her arms around Bob's legs, Sammie followed more slowly but also gave him a leg hug. "We waited and waited," Lizzie said loudly. "We had to put Hugo and Trixie and her babies in the garage 'cause we wanted to surprise you, and Trixie is gonna let Brandon have one puppy and Alexa wants the other one, and momma says that if its okay with you I gets to keep the other one. Is it?" asked Lizzie finally running out of breath.

"I'll talk to your momma," Bob promised Lizzie smiling, bending down to give her and Sammie a big hug.

Leeann was here, waiting for him. His heart had turned over when Lizzie had declared it home. With Leeann standing on the porch, he knew that the house was just a house unless loved ones dwelled there. For him, it would always be Leeann, whatever the future held.

Leeann walked slowly down the steps to put her arms around him in a warm clinging hug. He felt the pressure of her body all the way down to the tips of his toes. Surprise and desire ripped through him. He wanted to engulf her, but settled for putting his arm around her and pulling her close to his side. His insides smiled at the deep blush on Leeann's face.

"Come and meet my grandfather," she encouraged. "Grandfather Anderson, this is Bob Neal. Bob, my grandfather, John Anderson."

"How do you do," said the elderly gentlemen, shaking hands, looking the younger man over carefully.

"Truthfully I am so much better now that I'm home with all of you," Bob said honestly. He knew he was grinning foolishly but he couldn't stop the happiness from spilling out. His heart was overflowing with emotion.

"We're so glad you're home," Leeann said sending him warm, sidewise glances. "We've rather taken over your house though."

"I told you whatever you wanted to do would be absolutely fine with me," he chuckled. Protection, puppies, cars, money, love, a lifetime; what she wanted if was possible to give her, he would.

"Now that Louise and Hank are living in their little house, Catherine suggested that Grandfather come home with me. It seems that Ramsey women must have a guardian until they marry. Catherine told me that you are mine." She sent a flirty glance toward him, her eyes twinkling. "And I'm going to keep you."

"Which means that you and I need to talk after supper, son," sighed Mr. Anderson. "My grand-daughter insisted on coming home and needed a warrior, so I tagged along with Sean. He had to leave this morning. It's been a long time since those days' warrior days for me, the only aspect I've kept proficient is my ability with firearms."

"Sir, thank you for keeping everyone safe," Bob said sincerely. He knew that Hank was also around as potential backup.

Leeann took Bob's hand, clasping it tightly in hers. "Hank and Louise are waiting in the kitchen. They wanted to give us a chance to surprise you first. Dinner is almost ready, though.
Do you have a few minutes to talk, just you and me. Maybe go out to the barn?" Without waiting she instructed Lizzie, "You ring the bell when it's time for dinner."

Lizzie looked back and forth between them, then nodded her head in agreement.

" Ahhh, sure, I guess," Bob stammered. What in the world was so important that it needed to be said privately and immediately? He felt his back straighten a little as he prepared to deal with whatever was necessary for her.

They walked quickly to the barn, both knowing that the others were watching them.

As soon as they entered the warm, dim barn, Leeann rushed into his arms raising on her tiptoes to kiss him slowly and thoroughly.

"You promised that I could choose what I want. I choose you. I choose you as mine. Oh I've missed you so much," she murmured. "In your arms, I'm home. And I choose that you marry me."

EPILOGUE

Two years later

"If you let him fall, I'm not going to be happy," Leeann declared in a mock stern voice.

"You are kidding, right? Skye doesn't even need me except that his legs are too short to guide Nugget here," Bob laughed as he indicated his two-year-old son sitting in the saddle in front of him.

Nothing on earth pleased Bob more than watching his beautiful wife, not even his wonderful children. Contentment showed in his relaxed body and broad smile. The bonding between them was strong and true, a Ramsey woman with a mix of Anderson blood had mated with a Neal-Youngblood man. He knew in his heart that all of their families gone before were smiling from just beyond the misty veil.

Their bond had increased both of their artistic abilities and mingled their attributes. Leeann loved the multimedia wall art that she did, deriving great satisfaction in giving the prized pieces to friends and relatives. Bob painted less now, but his paintings had a special maturity and depth so they grew in popularity. He concentrated mostly on portraits running through his head; faces where truth of spirit could be exposed, fulfilling Grandfather Youngblood's prophecy.

Skye Neal looked very much his dad, even down to the right cheek dimple. His dark eyes and brows contrasted vividly with his platinum hair. He was built on the same large lines as his dad too, giving her holy hell with his nine-pound birth weight.

Lizzie sat on her pony, impatiently waiting for her dad and younger brother to come with her to ride over to the Paxton's house. She had developed into an excellent cowgirl, but her first love was still reading.

"You sure you don't want to go?" asked Bob, tugging on his cowboy hat. Immediately his daughter, Lizzie, pulled down her smaller replica, copying her dad's reaction.

"You've become quite a horsewoman," he coaxed Leeann.

"Nope, Silver has been fussy this morning and I finally got her down for a nap. Grandfather decided that he would also nap, so he can be close if she needs him." Grandfather Anderson divided his time between Shadow Valley and "down the hill" as he called it. He took his morning nap in a recliner near Silver's crib.

"Louise thinks she's teething and is hovering over both grandfather and Silver. Besides, if you decide to stay awhile, I'm going to need to feed her." Silver was their six-month old daughter with peach-fuzz auburn hair and big green eyes.

They had lost their other child, Sammie, the winter before. He had seemed fine when he went to sleep but did not wake up the next morning; slipping away as silently as he had lived. Lizzie still grieved for her silent partner and best friend.

After Sammie's death, Lizzie had decided that her new job was teaching Skye and Silver to read. So far her success rate had been limited. Six-month old Silver stuffed the paper in her mouth, ate the crayons, and threw up on Lizzie's shoes. When she could get Skye to sit down inside the house, he wanted to scribble all over the books, which Lizzy thought was a form of vandalism. She had declared both her siblings impossible, but she loved them anyway. She had told Leeann that Hugo and Trixie were better students.

The sturdy, two-year-old boy gave a wave, showing of tiny perfect teeth. "Mama, mama, watch," he demanded. "We go. Horse."

Dressed in fitted jeans, long sleeved tee shirt, and cowboy

boots, Leeann looked like a casual model for ranch wear. Full firm breasts, tiny body, and shoulder length multi-hued hair, she made Bob's mouth water and his jeans tighter.

Leeann blushed as she felt Bob's sexual interest in his gaze. Trying for some sort of calm, she reminded, "Don't forget to tell Deke about that stud getting out again and visiting our mares. He's too big for our little ladies."

"Nay. He's fine," he winked, making Leeann blush harder.

"Mama, mama. Baby," Skye announced pointing to a nearby corral where several mares stood. Sandy, one of Leeann's favorite mares to ride, was hanging over the fence.

"That's Sandy. Say Sandy," coaxed Bob to the toddler, pointing at the mare.

Skye frowned at his father in consternation. "No Sandy. No, no. Baby," he took Bob's hand and pointed it downward to Sandy's stomach area. "Dat baby," he announced happily. "Mine."

Wide-eyed Leeann stared at Bob who seemed as stunned as she was.

"No, damn it to hell! No!" Bob demanded with horror and disbelief in his soft voice.

Leeann gazed steadily at her soul-mate and their young son. "Whatever is his destiny, together we will deal with it. I'll call Catherine. And Kamon."